For more information on the author,
please visit her website:

www.TinaLuckett.com

THE SUITE TEA

NEMESIS

The Boss Moves Series – Book 2

TINA LUCKETT

Library of Congress: 2022921032

Publisher's Cataloging-in-Publication Data
Names: Luckett, Tina, author.
Title: The suite tea society / Tina Luckett.
Series: The Boss Moves Series.
Description: Van Buren Twp., MI: Lucketteer, 2022.
Identifiers: LCCN: 2022921032 | ISBN: 978-1-7364090-4-6
(paperback) | 979-8-3873420-0-4 (Amazon paperback) |
978-1-7364090-3-9 (ebook)
Subjects: LCSH Rich people—Fiction. | Friendship—Fiction. |
Crime— Fiction. | Detroit (Mich.)—Fiction. | Twenty-first
century—Fiction. | BISAC FICTION / Women | FICTION /
Thrillers / Crime | FICTION / City Life | FICTION / African
American & Black / Mystery & Detective | FICTION / Hispanic
& Latino
Classification: LLC PS3612 .U35 S85 2022 | DDC 813.6—dc23

Also available from Tina Luckett:

<u>The Boss Moves Series:</u>
The Suite Tea Society - Book 1
The Suite Tea Nemesis - Book 2
The Suite Tea Courtship - Book 3 (Coming Soon)

<u>Non-Fiction:</u>
The 7 Friendship Cycles (Coming Soon)

For my family,
Thank you for your support.
Love you all!

CONTENTS

ACT 1

GWEN'S NEMESIS

CHAPTER ONE

GWEN & TRINA

Gwen Didier had strayed from the conversation, but now she was alert at the mention of Greg's name.

"Are you okay, honey?" Robert asked with concern.

Gwen patted her lips with a napkin. "Yes. Did you say something about Lori's husband, Greg?"

"So, now you care about someone other than you?" Leah Didier asked snidely.

Ignoring her, Gwen looked to her husband. Every day with Leah around, Gwen was like a ticking bomb. One of these days, she was going to have to pull the woman by the hair and drag her out of her home. Since Leah knew she was in a tight corner with Gwen being pregnant, she took advantage of every opportunity to insult her. And Robert ignored her, especially now that she supposedly had cancer. The results were still pending, and Gwen hoped they were negative. "You mentioned something about Greg," Gwen repeated. There had been speculations about what had happened to him in the past two weeks since Greg had gone missing. At first, many thought he had gone on a trip with a bimbo as he did from time to time, but after his employees couldn't get through to him, the police were called in. To Gwen's knowledge, no progress had been made.

"Yes, I was talking with Wilson this morning," Robert said, referring to Greg's business partner.

"And?"

"Everyone's confused, including the police. It's like he fell off the surface of the earth. One morning, he called into work that he was going fishing. The guys at the lake never saw him. And the next, he's nowhere to be found. Literally vanished. Just unbelievable," Robert said with a bewildered look.

"He's probably in the arms of some slut," Gwen said. "You would know that, wouldn't you?" Leah asked.

Ignoring Leah, Gwen continued. "I wonder how Lori must feel." The women were polite with each other whenever they were in close proximity. At times, she watched Lori. Nothing seemed to have changed; she was still as dull as always. But Gwen couldn't be deceived. Behind that calmness was a beast. She never wanted to cross Lori's path. She had literally seen this woman hack her husband to pieces.

"She probably got rid of him. The police should be looking at her as their main suspect," said Blake, Robert's nephew. There were few people Gwen liked, and Blake was fortunate to be one. Perhaps their relationship was built on the foundation of their dislike for Leah.

"Blake!" his mother Rita shouted. She was a loud woman

who gave Gwen a headache just from the tone of her voice. Blake and his parents were in town after a month abroad, and Robert invited them for lunch. "Lori is a saint. She would never hurt a fly. As Gwen said, he must be with some other woman."

"The quiet ones are always crazy," Blake said, throwing a look at Leah.

Robert shook his head. "I don't think so. Sure, he may have run off to have a good time with another woman, but to leave behind the company and his money? That doesn't sound like the cocky Greg I know."

"Enough talk of them. Robert, how does it feel to be a father at your age, you lucky bastard?" Daniel, Blake's father, wasn't well-liked by many. He was creepy, and whenever he stared at Gwen, she itched to hit him with a shoe. He was a well-known drunk who'd cheated on Rita several times. It was well-known that he had only married her for her family's fortune.

Robert smiled at Gwen. "I'm indeed a lucky bastard."
"Oh!"

All eyes turned to Leah, who had her hand on her head. "Is everything all right?" Robert asked with concern.

"My head hurts. I should lie down. Will you walk me to my room?"

It irked Gwen that Leah was still in their lives. It was so infuriating! What sort of stupid bond did she and Robert have that he couldn't let go of?

"Don't worry, I'll help her to her room," Rita said, hurrying to the woman's side before throwing Gwen a pitying look.

Gwen relaxed.

After lunch, while the others shared a bottle of chardonnay, Gwen went on a walk with Blake.

"I thought you never wanted a brat," Blake said, looking at her stomach bump.

She was now in her second trimester, and her bump was getting bigger. "I didn't want one, but it was necessary."

"Leah." Blake nodded in understanding. "A smart decision, but it could cost you."

"What do you mean?"

"You don't understand, Leah."

"I do. She's an old bore who needs to get a life."

He flashed her a sad smile. "You see her that way, but she's worse than that. There's a lot about their past that you're not aware of. Don't for a moment think you've won. That woman may look weak and lonely, but she's a scheming bitch. She's crazy, and even I don't know what she's capable of. Never for a minute underestimate her."

"Leah?"

"Yes, Leah. She's a dangerous person and should not be taken lightly."

His words sent chills over Gwen's body. "What are you not telling me, Blake?"

"I—"

"Blake!" Rita called.

"Excuse me." Blake flashed her an apologetic smile as he hurried away. She knew she wouldn't get the opportunity to have this conversation again.

Gwen had always suspected there was more to Blake's dislike for Leah. He never voiced his opinion publicly, but he avoided her whenever possible. Many times, Gwen had caught him throwing dirty looks Leah's way. There was a story there, but she knew she wouldn't get answers from Blake. Did Robert know? He could be quite ignorant. What was the backstory Blake was referring to?

Gwen had always seen Leah as a harmless obstacle. She shook her head and placed her hand on her stomach. Blake was just being Blake, mysterious as always. He had no idea what he was saying. The Leah in there was a lonely old woman, and soon, she would be out of their lives for good, cancer or not.

TRINA

Trina Cantrell didn't meet the family of her past boyfriends until much later in her relationship. But here she was, staring at Charles Maxwell's sister. The woman stared back at her, probably trying to read her, just as Trina did the same.

Trina knew the woman was Charles's sister because she had the same bone structure as him. The only difference was that she was a lot shorter, barely five feet tall.

"Can I help you?" the woman asked with folded arms. "I'm here to—"

"Trina?" The door opened wider as Charles reached to hug her. "Who's that?" a voice asked from inside the house.

"Some lady!" Charles's sister yelled.

Charles led Trina into the living room, where seven more of his relatives were waiting. When Trina exchanged a look with him, she could swear he was holding back a laugh.

"Who's this, Charles?" an older woman asked. Her hair was totally gray, and she looked to be in her seventies.

"Grandma, this is my girlfriend, Trina," Charles said.

She couldn't recall the last time she had been introduced as someone's girlfriend. Errol might have, but it had been so long ago, that Trina couldn't remember.

Now, all eyes were on her with interest. Why on earth had she decided to drop by? Trina tugged her coat closer to her body, remembering she had nothing underneath it but a matching bra and panty set. Arrgghhh! She should've called first!

"Your girlfriend?"

The woman who stood at the kitchen doorway with a glass of wine had to be Charles's mother. Her eyes raked over Trina from top to bottom. Trina had been dating Charles for a couple of months, and it had been going well. They had lots of great conversation and fantastic sex. He was smart and a hard worker. Trina had also suspected he came from a successful black family. The man had manners, and it was apparent he hadn't grown up on the streets. He lived in a great apartment, had gone to college, and drove an expensive car. But Charles barely talked about his family. Glancing around the room, Trina noticed the women were well-dressed, and by owning a boutique, she could spot expensive jewelry when she saw it. As Charles's mother approached, Trina was sure the woman had undergone at least a couple of plastic surgeries. She was probably in her seventies, but she didn't look it.

"You are?" the woman asked as Trina got a whiff of her heavy perfume.

"Trina," she replied.

"I mentioned her to you, Mama," Charles said.

"I don't remember. Where did you go to school, Trina? Harvard?" the woman asked.

"Ha! No, I went to a Schoolcraft Community College." Everyone in the apartment became quiet. Now she was sure she had walked into a black version of the tea party club. She shared a look with Charles. He should've at least told her he came from a wealthy family.

"Oh. And what do you do?" his mother interrogated.

"I own a boutique and a co-work space," Trina said. She hated the vibes she was feeling. Trina felt like she was on a job interview with all the questions. She would take it easy; there was no need to flare up. Yet.

"So, you're a businesswoman. Interesting," his mother said, taking a sip from her glass.

"Umm… excuse us, everyone. I'll be back," Charles said, taking Trina's hand. He led her outside. "I'm sorry!"

She glared at him. "Why didn't you tell me your family was visiting?"

"To be honest, I didn't know you were coming over today."

"I was shocked to see so many people over, and I don't think your mother likes me much. I'm not a Harvard graduate, you know."

Charles grinned for an instant, but it disappeared under the intensity of her glare. "I'm sorry. It was a last-minute thing. Don't be mad. I don't want this to get between us. My mama is only looking out for me."

"I have to go. I thought I would come over here in my best lingerie, and we could have some fun, but you've got company." She opened her coat and gave Charles a quick peek.

His eyes widened, and she couldn't help but laugh. "Oh shit! I could send them all away."

They both knew he couldn't do it even as he said it. It was going to take some time for Charles's mother to warm up to her. She had read the situation in there, and she didn't like it one bit. Plus, she could tell Charles was a mama's boy, and Trina wasn't having any of it.

"Charles!"

They both turned toward the doorway. The light from above illuminated his mother. "Invite your friend to the barbecue."

"Mom, she won't be able to make it," Charles said quickly, throwing her a look to cooperate with him.

"What's more important than meeting your family?"

"She has an engagement on Sunday. Right?" Charles asked.

"I'm free on Sunday," Trina said. Charles sighed, obviously not pleased that she was able to make it.

"Good. Now say your goodbyes, Charles. We have a lot to talk about."

And like a seven-year-old, Charles kissed her goodbye.

Trina was pissed as she drove home. Even the ladies at the tea party had never looked down on her like that. The best thing she could have done was turn down the invitation, but her pride had refused to let her do so. She knew the dynamic of her relationship with Charles had just changed.

CHAPTER TWO

DANIELLE

Danielle O'Connell wasn't up for company, but Brad's mom, dad, sister, and cousin came to visit.

"You look different. Did you get a procedure done?" Martha asked. Brad's mother's compliment drew the attention of Brad's sister, Cindy, and his cousin, Jen.

"You do look different. What diet are you trying?" Cindy asked. "I'm not on a diet," Danielle said with a shrug.

"We know you don't like to share your secrets," Jen said with an eye roll.

Just then, Brad returned to the table. He had gone off to show his father a painting he had bought while in Seattle when he'd told Danielle he was in Texas. It was a hideous painting of a woman creepily cradling a baby. But Lawrence, the salesman, had called it art and claimed it would fetch more in the future.

"It's probably the new facial mask I'm using. It's a new line," Danielle said.

"That's probably it," Cindy agreed.

The so-called radiance they referred to had to do with her peace of mind. She'd had no idea how much the incident from years ago had a hold on her life. Looking back now, it was because of those pictures she had recoiled into a shell. Fear had made her live a quieter life than she'd wanted.

She felt a huge relief ever since her blackmailer was killed.

Everything seemed great, and she felt free.

"So, how has your little friend been?" Martha asked, a sad look overcoming her face.

"My little friend?" Danielle asked, confused.

"Lori, the one with the missing husband," Cindy clarified.

Oh, Lori. Danielle didn't like to be reminded of the woman. It made her shudder to think of what she had done to her husband. She had butchered him like she had no feelings. And the way she'd acted in the aftermath? Like the worried wife. Who would believe she had killed her husband and chopped him up into little pieces?

"Are you okay?" Martha asked.

"Yes." Danielle took a long sip from her glass.

"Lori was at our company today. There's a rumor she's going to be the new director," Brad said.

"What does she know about running a company? She's a woman! She will run that company into the ground. She should appoint a man to do the job, as it has always been done," her father-in-law, Mitch, stated. He was a pompous man who thought women should be at home or vacationing rather than in leadership.

Cindy glared at her father across the table, but the man

continued. "I don't know why Greg would just up and leave. He has more sense than that. He should return in a few days and have Lori back home."

"I think you're underestimating Lori," Danielle said. Mitch scoffed. "What can she do?"

Danielle smiled. *You have no idea*, she said silently. Everyone had underestimated Lori, and she had shocked them in the worst way possible. The longer Greg was missing, the deeper police would investigate, but she had a feeling Lori had covered all the loose ends, and nothing would be traced back to her.

"Excuse me, I have a call to take," Brad said, getting up.

Her eyes followed him as he left the room. Their love life seemed to be back, but it didn't feel the same. There was something wrong with them, and it certainly wasn't on her part. She could feel him holding back. She could feel something, but she didn't know what it was.

"Excuse me," she said. As she left the table, no one noticed her; their guests were too involved in their own conversations. She headed for the library where she knew he would be. The door wasn't completely shut, and she leaned in, listening to Brad.

"Hello, I'm sorry I can't come over this weekend. The wife is sick." After a pause. "You know how she is, honey. I know. I know. I'm sorry. I promise to make it up to you when I return." A pause. "I have to go now, love."

Danielle pulled away quickly, tears welling in her eyes. As much as she wanted to act like she'd heard wrong, she knew exactly what was happening. Brad was cheating on her! She hurried into the nearest powder room and locked the door. She stared into the mirror, tears now streaming down her face.

How could he do this to her? How long had this been going on? She thought back to the past several months. Brad's long absence from home, the impromptu meetings, and the innuendos dropped by his mother and sister now made sense.

She choked back a sob. She wanted to say she was wrong, but she knew deep down that his heart had been in another place for a while. How many people were aware of this? Did the other ladies know? Was she the only one who had been too stupid to see what was happening the entire time?

She wanted to remain in the powder room forever, but her presence was needed. She wanted to lash out at Brad, to yell at him and call him names, but what good would that do? His parents would defend him. Her family would tell her to deal with it, that men cheat, that there was nothing wrong with her husband and that she should remain a dutiful wife. But she loved Brad. She had devoted her life to being a great wife, and he had broken her trust.

What would Trina do? Would Trina cause a ruckus? No, she would act unaware, and in the meantime, she would scheme a way to control the situation. She patted her eyes dry and applied some powder to her face. Then, she returned to the living room.

"Danielle, where were you?" Brad asked as she took her place next to him.

"I went to the restroom. Are things okay with work?" she asked with a smile.

"Yes, they are," Brad returned a smile.

A sudden rage overcame her, and she clenched her table knife. She wondered if that was what Lori had felt as she chopped up her husband. The thought vanished, and she took a deep breath. She wouldn't let anger get the best of her. She was going to deal with this. Later in the afternoon, while Brad talked with his father about the company and the ladies lazed around in the living room, Danielle excused herself and went to her bedroom, claiming to have a headache.

Danielle: I think Brad is having an affair. Trina: What happened?

Danielle: I overheard him talking to someone. He used romantic endearments with her.

Gwen: I guess the cat is out of the bag, then. Danielle: You knew?

Gwen: You were the only one who believed your husband was off in Texas for work.

Danielle covered her face with her hand. How naive had she been?

She had been blind to her husband's philandering ways.

Danielle: Why did no one tell me?

Trina: Because we didn't want to hurt you.

Danielle: I'm hurt now. I consider you all my friends, and I wish you had told me.

Trina: It was a suspicion. We didn't have any proof. I'm going to call you now.

Her phone rang, and she hesitated before answering it. She felt betrayed by her friends. They should've told her the truth.

"I'm sorry we didn't tell you, Danielle, but we didn't want to burst your bubble of happiness."

"You should've told me! I feel like a fool now. Everyone has been laughing at me and throwing me pitying looks."

"Would you have felt better if we had told you? Would you have believed us? Or would you have cast us aside?" Trina asked.

Danielle sighed. The truth was, she probably would've cast them aside and avoided them. She had needed to personally witness Brad cheating to believe the fact that she had been glaring at her this whole time.

"What am I going to do now, Trina? I just feel so… broken." Tears brimmed in her eyes.

"We're going to handle this, Danielle, but I need you to take a deep breath. I can't promise your marriage will heal, but things will be okay for you."

Danielle took a deep breath. She hoped Trina was right because she had no idea how to deal with the loss she felt.

CHAPTER THREE

GABBY

Gabby Dodd laughed at the hilarious tale Trina just told her about meeting Charles's mom. Trina was pissed.

"I'm so glad Dave's mother isn't controlling. Those types of mothers can be quite annoying," Gabby said.

"Exactly! I know she didn't expect me to agree to come to their little party, and that's why I'm going to show up looking hot. I'm going to show her that she can't look down at me with her skinny ass."

"So, do you like this Charles dude?"

"Yes, he's nice and a complete gentleman."

"Well, then show up looking hot like you said. Make sure his mother knows she can't trample all over you," Gabby said, pulling a red gown from her closet. She had a dinner date with Dave tonight, and she was getting ready.

"Sorry, Gabby, I have to go now. My other line is ringing. Talk to you later."

"Later then." As Gabby hung up, someone knocked on her bedroom door. It was Lisa, the head maid. She had been with Dave's family since before Gabby married Dave.

"You have a visitor," Lisa informed.

Visitors didn't drop by uninvited. She wasn't a busy woman, but that didn't mean she entertained guests without prior notice.

"Who is it?" she asked.

Lisa sighed. "I think you need to see for yourself."

Curious, she went downstairs. In the living room sat a slender woman who looked like she had just walked off a beauty pageant stage. Her skin was so smooth she looked like a doll. Diamond studs were placed on both ears. Seated next to her was a boy of about ten years old.

She looked at Lisa questioningly. Was she supposed to know this woman? "Who are you?" she asked.

When the woman stood up, Gabby envied her tiny waist. "I'm Diana."

"Okay?"

"I'm the mother of Dave's child," the woman said with a nod at the boy.

The world instantly faded around Gabby. The furniture. Lisa.

The woman. Everything. "Ma'am?" Lisa said.

She snapped out of her dazed state, and reality set in. "What did you just say?"

"Adrian."

The boy perked up at this. "Mother?" he asked in a British accent. With her hands on his shoulder, Diana said, "This is

Adrian. He's Dave's son."

Gabby mustered a chuckle. "So, you come into my home and announce this is my husband's son? And I'm supposed to believe you?" Gabby asked.

"Isn't it obvious?"

Indeed, it was. She had seen pictures of Dave as a child. This child was a replica of him. He had those piercing dark eyes and a bony facial structure.

"You should leave," Gabby said.

"I wasn't planning on staying. Yet. Tell Dave when he comes home that I dropped by with his son. We'll be back." She looked down at the child. "Let's go, Adrian. Daddy isn't home." She flashed Gabby a quick smile as she took the boy's hand.

"Do you need a drink, ma'am?" Lisa asked.

"Yes. Please make it a double scotch," Gabby said in a tiny voice she couldn't recognize.

She felt faint as she dropped into a seat. Dave had a son! At least the child wasn't a product of adultery. He looked ten at most; he must have been born before she'd met Dave. Perhaps a result of an old relationship. But why now? Why had the woman resurfaced to disrupt her life?

She grabbed the glass from Lisa's hand and tossed the contents into her mouth. Then she handed it back, hurried to her bedroom, and collapsed on the bed. She wanted to cry, to scream, but she did none of that. She just lay in bed, lost in her thoughts.

Hours must have gone by before she heard the bedroom door open. Dave's presence filled the space.

"Gabby? Why are you not dressed? We have a reservation at seven." "Diana dropped by," Gabby said, watching him as she sat up on

the bed.

He stiffened at the mention of the name. "Diana?"

"She came with a child. Your son," she continued in a drowsed state.

"Diana? I have a son?" he asked, realizing what she had said. He settled down on the bed, his face buried in his hands.

"Who's Diana?" Gabby snapped.

He flinched at her question. "I… Diana and I were friends, and we started dating in college. We dated for years. She was… amazing." Her heart squeezed at the tenderness in his voice. It was clear he still had feelings for the woman. If he had cared for her, what would

have happened between them?

"And then we got into a fight—or more like I cheated. It was a mistake!" Dave quickly defended.

Why did Gabby feel glee that he had cheated on Diana even if it had been wrong of him?

"When she found out, she ended things between us. She refused to listen to me and just left. I went to her apartment one morning, and it was empty. She'd disappeared, and none of her family or friends would tell me her whereabouts. I didn't know we had a son. I didn't even know she was pregnant. Why didn't she tell me? Why would she keep him away from me?" Dave wondered aloud.

"Do you still love her?" Gabby asked. "No!" he said rather too quickly.

Gabby lifted a brow. Yes, he still loved her. It seemed like a bowl of cold water had been thrown on her.

"Did she leave a number? An address?" Dave asked with excitement.

She wondered if he was more excited about the prospect of having Diana back in his life or the knowledge that he had a son.

"Where are you going?" Gabby asked as Dave headed to the door. "To get my son."

The moment the door closed behind him, she burst into tears. In the past two years, she had suffered two miscarriages, one of which Dave wasn't aware of. She loved children. As a teenager, she babysat children in the apartment block. She didn't have siblings, but she had always dreamed of having her own children running around her home. She yearned to be a loving mother, different from the one she had while growing up. Whenever she saw a parent with their child, her heart ached to have one of her own. She had even offered Alicia, one of the ladies at the tea party, her services to babysit if the help was ever needed. And she would offer the same to Gwen, even if the woman would rather surround herself with nannies. It was unfortunate that she longed for children but didn't have any.

Gabby was supposed to be the mother to Dave's child, not Diana, who still seemed to occupy a place in his heart.

Their marriage was going to change drastically with the appearance of Diana and her son. They were supposed to celebrate tonight, but her husband was out looking for his son. As she curled up in bed, she was consumed by fear for her future.

CHAPTER FOUR

TRINA

Charles's parents, Charles Sr. and Brenda Maxwell, lived in a large house in a black-dominated, upper-district neighborhood. Trina was no stranger to these parts. While she was growing up, the neighborhood had always been attributed to money. It was occupied by successful black doctors, lawyers, politicians, etc. The houses here cost millions, and the owners drove luxurious vehicles.

"My family can be quite much."

Charles had picked Trina up from her house. He looked dashing as always with his locks in a bun. He had been quiet most of the ride, and she could sense his discomfort. It was either he didn't want her around his family because he was embarrassed by her or he was scared of what they would do to her.

"Don't worry; I'm a big girl. I can take care of myself," Trina said with a shrug. It would take more than a fancy house, college degrees, and all that shit to make her think less of herself. Mingling with the tea ladies, who were much wealthier than her, had made her realize money wasn't all that. Even though they were rich, they could also be crazy and have many problems.

There were several cars parked in the driveway with valets directing them. He kissed her briefly before they got out of the car and held her hand as they walked into the house. A few people were in the living room, and Charles showed her around, making quick introductions. The dirty and curious looks she received from mostly the women didn't escape her notice. She could literally smell the wealth and pompousness among them.

She loved the decor. High walls and dark wood—it was a perfect combo. Her eyes drifted to a shelf filled with degrees and awards. The Maxwells were a bunch of high achievers.

"Is that you?" she asked, giggling as her eyes rested on a picture of Charles as a baby.

He grinned. "I made a good-looking baby, right?" "An innocent one," she bantered back.

"Hi, Charles and Tammy," his mother, Brenda, said, joining them. Her slender shape was encased in a beautiful brown dress. Trina quickly made a mental note to get a cheaper version for the boutique.

"It's Trina, Mom," Charles corrected.

His mother dismissed him with a wave of her hand. "Let's go outside. There's someone I'm sure you'll be happy to see," Brenda said, taking her son's hand and leading him away.

Charles threw Trina an apologetic look. She followed behind in an amused state. Could the woman make it more obvious that she didn't want Trina around?

More guests occupied a huge backyard. A swimming pool was off to the side, but a couple of children only occupied it. Brenda led her son to a white gazebo, one of the few that littered the backyard.

"Dad!"

Charles's father was a tall man with a kind face, which immediately put Trina at ease. He reminded her of her literature teacher back in high school. Trina hadn't understood anything he taught, but he'd given her good grades even if she had been horrible at the tests.

"Dad, this is Trina, my girlfriend," Charles introduced.

The older man shook her hand firmly, giving her a thorough once-over. Charles had told her his father was a retired surgeon. She had googled his name, and hell was he successful. He was one of the first black doctors to own his own private clinic, and he was on the board of various institutions. It was then she berated herself for not searching Charles on the internet before they had started dating, not that it would've made any difference, except she would've been more prepared. He came from a successful, respected, and wealthy family. Trina had mingled with rich white folks, and now she was with her black folks.

"It's great to meet you, Trina. Welcome to our home," his father said.

"Charles?"

They both turned toward the voice. The moment Trina's eyes rested on the woman, she knew she was going to be major trouble. She looked like she could be a politician's wife.

Her blue blouse was tucked into a blue denim skirt, and her hair was neatly sleeked back. There wasn't a blemish on her brown skin. And that body, did she even eat anything other than vegetables?

"Michelle? When did you return?" Charles asked as he hugged her.

"She returned a few days ago, and I called her mother and informed her they both needed to be here," Brenda said happily. She turned to Trina. "Michelle is Charles's childhood friend. They've been friends forever. Do you know she's a doctor? She's been in South Africa helping sick children."

"I returned a few days ago. I know I should've called you,"

Michelle said as Trina wrapped her arms around her man. The woman's eyes flashed at her, and Trina grinned. Oh yes, little miss Michelle wasn't as innocent as she seemed.

"Michelle, this is Trina, my girlfriend. Trina, I don't know if I mentioned Michelle—"

"You never did." Trina shook her head.

"I can't believe I forgot Michelle is an old friend of mine," Charles said.

"It is nice to meet you, Michelle. Any friend of Charles is a friend of mine," Trina said.

"What do you do? Are you a doctor? A lawyer?" Michelle asked. "Trina runs her own business. A bakery, right?" Brenda asked. "No, ma'am, I run a successful clothing boutique off 8 Mile Road.

Michelle, you should stop by sometime."

Michelle looked at her disgustedly; however, the look quickly dissolved. Trina's smile remained, despite Brenda calling her boutique a bakery. Who the hell did Brenda think she was?

"Charles, why don't you show Michelle your father's new art collection? The African collection. With her recent travel, I suppose Michelle should be familiar with it," Brenda suggested.

"Umm… Trina?" Charles turned to her.

"Don't worry, I'll take good care of her," his mother said, placing a hand on Trina's shoulder.

Trina's smile wavered as Michelle wrapped her arms around Charles as they walked away.

Brenda pulled away from her. "I'm sure you can entertain yourself in some way."

And with that, the older woman left her to join her laughing guests. Trina grabbed a glass of wine from a passing waiter and took a long sip, followed by a deep breath. She had just been passed a message by Charles's mother. She didn't want her for her son. She wanted a well-educated woman like Michelle, the doctor.

Things were not serious with Charles yet, but that didn't mean Trina was going to accept defeat and walk away. She was going to stick around for much longer. She couldn't give Brenda the victory nor allow that scheming, thin bitch to have her man.

Trina left the gazebo. She had come for the party, after all, and she wasn't going to let her mood be soiled.

"Trina?" a deep, pleasant voice said from a distance.

Trina's mouth fell open, and she laughed. "Denzel Coleman?

What the hell?"

Strong arms enveloped her, and she realized how much she needed that hug. He pulled away from her, wearing a surprised look. "Of all places, Trina, I didn't expect to see you here," Denzel said.

The feeling was mutual. Years ago, when she had been in college, Denzel had been one of the professors. He had taught a couple of her classes, and she had worked directly under him on a project. He was so handsome. All 6'2" of chocolate, with beautiful eyes and pearly white teeth, he had been the youngest on the school board. He had told her his parents were overachievers, and he had gotten into college in his early teens. It had been no surprise that many ladies had thrown themselves at him.

He had hit on her several times, but she had turned down his advances. She hadn't wanted to be caught in a situation where she would end up being at the mercy of someone else. If things had gone sour between them, he could've held her grades against her. As much as she had found Denzel hot, she knew when not to cross the line. It had been years since she had last seen him. He had left before her graduation; rumor was he had left the country after one of his students filed sexual harassment charges against him.

"Damn! You look good as always, Trina," Denzel said, his eyes roving over her.

She rolled her eyes playfully. He was a tease, as always. "What are you doing here?"

"This is my aunt's home," Denzel said with a shrug. Wait! Was Brenda his aunt? Which meant— "Denzel!"

With Denzel's arms around Trina's waist, they both turned.

Charles appeared surprised to see her with his cousin.

"Denzel!" Michelle smiled—a smile Trina easily read. The woman had better make a decision instead of having the hots for both men.

"Hey, cuz! How're you doing? Want to introduce you to my old friend," Denzel said with a wide grin.

"Why am I not surprised?" Michelle sneered.

"Umm, Denzel, I'm here with Charles. He's my boyfriend," Trina said.

Denzel froze. Then he burst into laughter. "This is fucking lit! You're dating Trina? You are one lucky dude! You know, she turned me down every time I asked her out. What you got that I don't have?" His eyes lowered to his cousin's pants.

Trina swatted him. He had gotten even worse over time. Denzel squeezed her.

"Welcome to the family, Trina," he said with a broad smile. "Charles!" Brenda joined them, followed by another woman

Trina recalled seeing at Charles's apartment that night. "Did you show Michelle the collection?"

"Yes, I did," Charles said. Brenda's eyes shifted between the men as they stood by Trina's side. Trina pushed back a chuckle.

"Denzel, you're here," Brenda said annoyedly.

"My favorite aunt in the world. What do you think of Trina? Isn't she amazing? And hot?" he added with a wink that made Trina giggle.

"You know her?" Brenda asked.

"She was one of my students at Schoolcraft College. One of the smartest," he added with pride.

"I see." Brenda's eyes sparked with fury now. Trina had a feeling the woman disliked her even more.

"Charles, your father wants to see you," Brenda said. "Leave the girl behind. Your cousin can entertain her. Come along, Michelle," Brenda called as she stormed off with Charles and Brenda.

"My aunt doesn't like you," Denzel said.

"She doesn't seem to like you either." Trina smiled. Denzel had never acted like he came from wealth. He was the bad boy who drove an old truck and smoked weed. Yet, he had to be smart to graduate college so young and be a professor.

"Cheers to that!" Denzel said, handing her a wineglass from a passing waiter. Their glasses clinked with a cheer.

The once dull party turned into a delight for Trina. Denzel stuck to her side, giving her tidbits of information about the guests. As expected, Michelle came from a respected family, and Brenda wanted Charles to get married to her, although Charles saw her as a little sister. His mother, however, didn't care. Charles's sisters had married off well, and as her only son, he was going to do the same.

Denzel was the black sheep of the family. His parents had learned to deal with this, but not his aunt, who was highly disappointed that he decided to live his life recklessly without order. When he left Schoolcraft College, he went to Barbados, where he lived by the sea and taught children during the weekdays. From there, he went to Cuba. It was the same routine with him: traveling, teaching, and screwing around, to his family's horror. He had only returned to the States a few months ago when his mother fell ill.

"You know you're in for a long ride with Charles," Denzel warned as they settled down under a gazebo. "Brenda is not going to let you entrap her son."

"Entrap?" she asked, amused. He gave her a look, and she laughed heartily, earning a few glances.

"You know what I mean, Trina. You're the type of woman who's going to tie a man down, make him give you everything. The type of woman who won't let his mama control him. Brenda loves control. She thrives on it. Pardon me, but you're not from around here. You don't have enough money, no fancy degree, and all that shit. And she doesn't want that. She wants a—"

"A classy woman, right? I kind of peeped that," Trina said. "With Brenda, there's no negotiation. She's going to get you out of the equation. So, are you going to run for the hills?"

"Why? Where's the fun in that?"

Denzel grinned. "I knew there was a reason I liked you."

CHAPTER FIVE

GWEN

Gwen happily ate the piece of ham Gabby had refused to eat. Looking around the table, she seemed to be the only one in a happy mood. The others wore long faces. Poor girls.

"So, Gabby, do you need a good divorce lawyer? I know one. He helped my cousin, and she got a huge alimony," Gwen said.

"Gwen!" Trina glared.

"What? It's going to happen. Everyone knew how devastated Dave was when Diana left him. It was then he started drinking and visiting the clubs," she added with a look at Gabby. People didn't discuss it because they knew where they had met—at a strip club, not that Gwen was judging her.

"Don't mention her name again," Gabby snapped. "You'll be hearing more of her," Gwen said.

She had given the ladies a quick rundown of Dave's relationship with Diana. Diana was a sweetheart that everyone had liked—well, except Gwen. She was just too pretty and all smiles; it made Gwen want to puke. She had been a beauty queen with brains. The one every mother wanted their daughter to associate with. Her family had once been wealthy, but bad investments had left them with nothing but their name and connections. Everyone had known she would marry well—probably into politics with how well-mannered Diana was with her never-faltering smile. So, it was no surprise when she ended up with Dave, a judge's grandson, and a politician's son.

"You know they were the 'power' couple, right?" Gwen asked. They'd looked so sweet and mushy together. And then Dave ruined things. He cheated, and Diana dumped his ass. She left after that, with everyone pissed at Dave for messing things up. Gwen had forgotten about Diana until her return.

"What has Dave said?" Trina asked.

Gabby sighed. She was a pretty girl–Dave obviously liked them pretty and innocent looking. She also had a great fashion sense.

"He met with her two days ago. We haven't sat down to discuss anything else. I'm just... this is just so devastating. I...."

"You could have given him a baby all this while, and you would have no worries," Gwen said.

Gabby burst into tears, surprising everyone at the table. "Umm... Gabby, I didn't mean it," Gwen said as Trina shot her a dirty look.

"I've had two miscarriages," Gabby said as she dabbed her eyes with a napkin.

For the first time, Gwen felt like shit. Her hand quickly went to her stomach. She couldn't imagine losing the baby. That would be so horrible! As much as the baby was a burden, she was getting used to having it around and looking forward to being a mother.

"I'm sorry, Gabby," she said with sincerity.

Trina hugged Gabby tightly, with Danielle placing a hand over hers.

"I wanted to be the one to give him children and…. You know what, I don't even care that he has a son. But this woman, she's going to be trouble. I know it. I can feel it. She isn't just back to reunite father and son. She's…."

Gwen had to agree with her. It didn't seem that way, either. Diana was back to take Gabby's man.

"I don't know what I'm going to do. I love Dave. If this marriage ends, it's going to kill me," Gabby said.

"You need to start with getting a divorce lawyer," Gwen suggested. Gabby looked away. "Umm… I signed a prenup, so…."

The table went completely quiet.

"You fucking signed a prenup? Are you crazy?" Trina yelled.

While it was rather bold of Trina, Gwen had to agree with her. A prenup? That was stupid! With Gabby's background, she should've been smarter than that. What did people like her say when they married wealthy men? Secure the bag. This woman had totally lost the bag.

"I wanted him to trust me. Trust that I wasn't marrying him for his money," Gabby defended.

"Oh, Gabby. What have you done?" Trina groaned.

"So, you basically get nothing if you divorce him?" Danielle asked, surprised.

"Well, there's a specified sum. But I don't think Dave would leave me empty-handed if we got divorced," Gabby said.

While Gwen didn't think so either, if Diana were in the picture and insisted on it, he would leave her without a glance back.

"Now more than ever, you need to start saving up whatever you can get, Gabby. Otherwise, you're going to be abandoned on the pavement with nothing. Girl, I thought you were smarter than that," Trina said before taking a long drink from her glass.

"I think we're overthinking this," Danielle added. "No one is divorcing anyone."

"Yet," Gwen cut in.

"We're just assuming things. He may just be excited to be a father, and that's all. I think you need to have a heart-to-heart with Dave," Danielle continued.

Gwen chuckled. "Like the one you had with your husband?"

Danielle glared at her. "As I was saying, you need to talk to Dave and figure out what to do with the child. Things like this happen, right? You can deal with this together, and there doesn't have to be a divorce." She looked to Trina for support.

"While we should still consider the possibility of divorce with how shady this Diana seems, Danielle is right. Dave respects you a lot. You have to talk to him about the boy,"

Trina said.

"Being married to you doesn't stop him from being a father. They can have joint custody, right?" Danielle asked.

"While this sounds rosy, you won't be able to hold it for much longer. If Dave still has feelings for Diana, you can't stop him from cheating. This will only bring them closer, and soon you're out of the marriage and living in a motel," Gwen said.

"Ignore Gwen. Just talk to Dave first. Stop giving him the silent treatment. This isn't his fault. She was an ex who returned to his life," Danielle said.

"So, Danielle the shrink, when will you confront your husband?" Gwen asked. She smiled as Danielle went pale.

"This isn't about me!" "Really?"

Danielle sighed. "Fine! I don't know what to do. Happy now? My husband is cheating, and I don't know what to do!" Now she was crying, with tears streaming down her face.

Gwen groaned. What was wrong with the ladies today? Why were they being so emotional? Her eyes rested on Trina. Was she going to cry too?

As if reading her mind, Trina said, "Don't even think about it.

Listen, everyone! No tears. If there's anyone who should be crying, it should be Gwen, whose hormones are in a twist."

"Hey!"

"Gabby, you're going to do as we agreed. Sit down and talk to your husband. Danielle, you either confront your husband or keep quiet and continue to condone his cheating while you grow to hate him. The ball is in your court," Trina said. "Now, which of you has an annoying mother-in-law?"

Gwen raised a hand, and her eyes rested on Trina "Not Robert. Thankfully, his mother was dead long before I came into the picture." She shuddered to imagine the wrinkles she would've gotten if she had to fight off his mother and Leah at the same time. "I once dated this man whose mother was sent from hell, but I put her in her place."

"Good, I need some tips. I need to nail this woman," Trina said, leaning forward.

Gwen was more than happy to oblige her. After all, she seemed like the only one with an amazing life.

CHAPTER SIX

GABBY

Gabby and Dave were seated out on the patio. She had called him a few hours ago while he was at the office and told him they needed to talk. It seemed like forever since they had sat outside together. When he had been home, she'd been giving him the silent treatment these past few days. It hurt her to see him so excited to be a father, but she couldn't stop him from being one.

"What are you going to do with the child?" Gabby asked.

"I know the situation is not one anyone would be pleased with. But Adrian is my son, and I have missed almost a decade of being his father. I have to make up for it."

She noticed how tired he was. It certainly hadn't been easy for him. She tried to put herself in his shoes and imagined having a child resurface after so many years. Yeah, it had taken a toll on him.

"And I have no issue with that. Both of you deserve to be in each other's lives," Gabby said. "Adrian wasn't to blame.

He's innocent in all of this. He's the child. What about Diana?"

"What about her?" Dave frowned.

"She never told you about your son. That was cruel of her." All Gabby had heard so far were praises about the woman and how much of a darling she was. But in her opinion, any woman who could deny a child the presence of his father for that long was a horrible person.

"I… I hurt her. I cheated on her," Dave defended.

"But that doesn't make what she did right. Why is she resurfacing now?" Gabby asked.

"She felt it was time I know my son, and he knows me. She realized what she had done was wrong," Dave said.

Indeed. "And what arrangements are you making with her? Shared custody?" she asked.

Dave sighed. "Diana doesn't want shared custody. She will be going back to England with Adrian."

Relief settled in her. Great! Diana needed to return to where she'd come from.

"But I can't let her leave. I have missed many years. I've always envisioned that I'd be present in my child's life. I don't want to be one of those fathers who talks to his child once a month and sees them once a year. I want to teach my child how to play baseball. I want him to take over the family business one day."

"Then try to convince her to stay." Gabby couldn't believe she was saying this. The right thing to do was make sure the woman was out of their lives, but she couldn't be selfish. Dave's happiness was also important to her.

"That's what I'm trying to do. I'm sorry if I've been cold in any way. It's just been a difficult blow to deal with," Dave apologized, reaching for her.

She went to him and rested her head on his shoulder. "It's going to be all right."

"I hope so. I've spoken to Drew," he said, referring to his friend who was an attorney.

"What did he say?"

"Custody might be difficult if I'm not on the child's birth certificate. I asked Diana, and she told me she didn't put my name on it," Dave said. "You know, I'm trying not to be angry, but I can't believe she would hide such news from me, even if we were done…. I guess I hurt her more than I thought I did."

There was more he wanted to say; she could feel it lingering. What had really happened between them? Dave wasn't the type of person to cheat in a happy relationship. Something must have triggered him to cheat on this supposedly amazing woman. But would he share that with her?

"What if I talk to her?" Gabby suggested. Dave pulled away from her. "Talk to her?"

Gabby nodded. "Yes, woman to woman. Maybe I can convince her to have Adrian stay." He was going to be Gabby's stepson, and she would shower him with love, just as she would her own child.

"You would do that for me?" Dave asked.

"I would do anything for you." This incident made her realize how much she loved Dave, and she couldn't imagine a life without him. In the beginning, she felt gratitude toward him for pulling her out of a life of poverty, but he was so easy to love, and she didn't want to lose what they had.

"I'll give you her phone number," Dave said, reaching for his phone.

"Don't worry; I know where to find her."

Everyone knew where Diana stayed—at the S Hotel in the heart of Detroit Downtown. Many of the people in their social circle loved having a cocktail in the hotel's sprawling living room.

The following day, Gabby handed her car keys to the valet and made her way into the vast foyer of the hotel. She approached the front desk to place a call to Diana's room. She knew how awkward this was going to be, but she needed to give it a try.

Just as the woman at the front desk was about to place the call, Gabby saw Diana and Adrian, along with a woman she wasn't surprised to see. From the moment Diana returned, Amanda had leeched herself to her.

"Diana!" Gabby called, earning looks as she walked toward the women.

"Giselle, what are you doing here?" Diana asked.

Ignoring the deliberate name slip, Gabby said, "I would like to talk to you. Alone," she added for Amanda's benefit.

"Well, I'm busy, so I have only a few moments to spare. I have to see Amanda off and then ensure Adrian is occupied," Diana said.

"I'll be waiting." Gabby nodded at the armchairs that littered the lobby.

She waited for almost an hour. She knew this was a deliberate waste of her time, but she decided to be patient. Her anger would yield no results. She was here on Dave's behalf, after all.

"I have time for you now," Diana announced, standing before her.

She followed the woman outside to the poolside, under the shade.

It was quiet, giving them some privacy.

"What do you want to talk about?" Diana asked, glancing at her wristwatch.

"It is about Adrian and Dave. I know you want to return to England, but I want you to allow Dave to raise his son in the U.S. He really wants to be in his son's life," Gabby said softly, hoping she would be able to talk some sense into her.

Diana laughed. "Don't tell me you're that naive," she said in a cold voice, different from the tender voice of earlier. "Gabby, you seem like a darling, sweet and all that—although, I have no idea what Dave sees in you. And, yes, I know your background." Her eyes drifted from the top of Gabby's head downward. "I don't think I was clear last time. I returned to give Adrian a family—a family consisting of his father and mother—and you are certainly not in the picture."

"I—"

"I can read you, Gabby. You're here out of insecurity. I'm sure your little friends have told you all about Dave and me. I'm taking him back."

"You really do have a high opinion of yourself, don't you?" Gabby glared. She had known the woman's sweetness was all an act.

"I do, and everyone does as well. Look, I'm not going to allow some other woman to play mother to my son. Never! Adrian deserves to live with respectable parents and not with a woman of questionable character. And think twice before saying Dave loves you. He loves me as well, and when I give him an ultimatum to choose you or his son, we both know what he'll do. You want to know why I'm telling you this? So, you don't bother wasting your time, Gabby. I'm back, and you're out. Now, excuse me bitch."

Gabby resisted the strong urge to slap her in the face. She sat there for a moment in a frozen state; she needed time to gather the strength to move. Diana had not returned to reconcile father and son. She had returned to destroy her marriage. But Gabby wasn't giving Dave up without a fight. She pulled her phone from her purse.

Gabby: 911. The S Hotel. I need you all. Trina: Be there in 10 minutes.

Danielle: I'm on my way.

Gwen: What is this all about? Never mind. I guess I can roll myself out of bed. I'll be there as soon as I can.

CHAPTER SEVEN

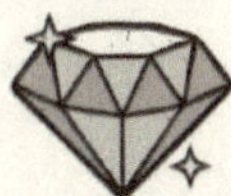

TRINA, GWEN, & DANIELLE

Trina hated the state Gabby was in. She had consumed almost a bottle of scotch and was still ruffled, but what did she expect? The woman had just been threatened by her husband's baby mama. Trina hadn't even seen this Diana woman, but she disliked her already. She had left the man ten years ago and returned to take her place like she had never left. What kind of entitled woman did that? Hell no!

"I think my feet are getting swollen." Gwen grimaced as she tried to shove her feet into a pair of shoes. The saleswoman stood next to her, looking terrified. Gwen had terrorized the poor employee from the moment they'd walked in. Trina didn't succumb to pity shopping, but with how miserable Gabby felt, she had no other option.

"Get me another pair," Gwen snapped at the saleswoman, who was glad to escape them. "I really can't wait for this baby to come out!" Gwen rubbed her protruding stomach.

Sighing, Gabby dropped the red dress she had picked off the rack. "I really don't feel like shopping anymore. I want to go home and climb into bed."

"Gabby, I need you to snap out of this and start figuring out a way to save your marriage," Trina said. Aside from the fact her friend's social standing was going to fall, Gabby and Dave made a great couple, and Trina didn't want that to end any time soon.

"I don't think my marriage can be saved," Gabby said dejectedly. That was the mistake Gabby was making. Even though Dave could still be in love with his ex, that didn't mean he was going to divorce Gabby. On the other hand, with Diana dangling their son as collateral, Dave might be cornered and have no other choice.

"But why did she wait this long just to return and try to destroy the life he's built?" Danielle said to herself.

They needed to find out more about Diana. The woman was quite confident, and people like her had skeletons in their closet. If they found something to hold against her, then they could manipulate the situation to their own benefit.

"I don't know," Gabby started when Trina voiced her opinion. "What if we get her angry, and she leaves with Adrian? Dave would be angry with me."

"So, you would rather she takes everything from you?" Gwen asked.

Gabby sighed. "I think I'm going crazy. I hate what's going on. I just...."

"What about Dave's parents?" Trina asked. Perhaps they could be of help. She knew a heart attack had made Dave's father retire from politics. According to Gabby, Clifford lived a sedentary life and had to use a cane. Dave's mother, Moira, also lived a quiet life and was on the board of several charities.

"Don't even involve them. They'll be no help. Dave's father totally adores Diana, and so does his mother," Gwen warned.

"But they like me too," Gabby interjected.

"We should find out about Diana. I'm sure there will be something for us to use." Trina's attention was drawn to movement at the door, and she sighed.

Of all places to run into Charles's mother and Michelle, it had to be here. The two women, along with two others, had just walked into the luxurious shop. There was no place to hide—not that she would do such a thing. Why would she hide from them?

Brenda's eyes rested on her in surprise, then on her companions. As she approached, Trina wondered what was going through her mind.

"Trina, it's a surprise to see you here. This doesn't seem like your scene," Brenda said, taking a second look at her companions.

"Brenda, how are you?" Trina asked sweetly.

"Is this Charles's mother?" Gwen asked with interest.

Trina threw her a look, beseeching her to behave. Brenda looked surprised that Gwen was aware of who she was.

"Trina has told us so much about you," Gwen continued.

"Hi, Danielle. How are you and Brad doing? I haven't seen you since your wedding reception." Brenda asked Danielle as Michelle joined them.

"Hello, Brenda. Brad and I are doing great. I will let him know that I bumped into you today."

"Please do and tell your mother I said hi for me. Is Trina a friend of yours?" Brenda asked.

"Yes, Trina is a good friend of mine," Danielle said as she handed her card to the saleswoman.

"I see you love climbing up the social ladder," Michelle chipped in. "Is this the bitch you mentioned?" Gwen sneered.

Trina's eyes widened. Hell no! Gwen! As much as she was shocked by Gwen, she was impressed. She was going to high-five her later.

"It was nice seeing you, Brenda, but we have to get going now," Trina said as she pulled Gwen to the counter to finalize her shopping. She could feel the women's glares at them. She was pretty sure she had gone further upon their blacklist.

"Well, she's kind of pretty, but you could win in a fight, right?" Gwen asked as they headed out of the shop.

"She reminds me of Diana," Gabby muttered, her mind on her marriage crisis, of course.

"Do you think I should hire a PI to find out who Brad is cheating with?" Danielle wondered aloud.

Trina whirled around. "Enough with the bitching!" She was tired of the depressing situations they were all in. Danielle was still coming to terms with her husband possibly being a serial cheater. Gabby had a scheming baby mama trying to replace her in her own marriage, and Trina was having a mama's boy issue while Gwen was taking delight in their messed-up situations.

Trina's relationship with Charles had been somewhat

strange since the party. The ride back home had been silent. She sensed he'd been pissed that she had spent the party by Denzel's side, but what had Charles expected when he couldn't be free of Michelle for even a moment. They talked on the phone regularly, but there was a certain tension, and they hadn't seen each other since then. She couldn't afford to lose to Brenda. If she broke things off, it would be on her terms and not because Brenda forced her out.

"So, how soon can we start looking for information on Diana?" Gabby asked.

GWEN

Gwen returned to a quiet home. There was no Leah and her horrible face. Neither was there a Robert.

"They went out for lunch," the butler informed her with a frown.

"What happened?"

He hesitated before answering. "They went out to have lunch. I believe cancer was found in Leah's test."

Gwen let loose a frustrated sigh. She had been hoping the results would turn out that Leah was healthy. They had been waiting for days now. This was just great! She knew Robert would want to be there for his so-called friend.

She shoved her bags at the butler and stomped to her room. Leah was certainly not going to steal her shine. It was cancer and not the end of the world. Heck! Having a child was more important than someone having cancer. It was bringing in a new life versus going out with the old. She would be glad to see the woman leave them for good. At least, the most Robert would do was drop flowers at her grave site.

She was on the patio when they arrived. Robert held Leah, who wore a hideous flowing gown with a turban over her head. Gwen's eyes raked over her as if looking for the cancer. Leah did look a little frail, Gwen had to admit.

Robert let go of Leah instantly to kiss Gwen and caress her stomach. She felt a stir in her abdomen.

"The results came back," he said, returning to Leah's side. "I have cancer," Leah said.

Gwen shrugged, and Leah's face fell, clearly not the expression Leah had expected. "One way or another, you die."

"Gwen! Leah is not going to die. She'll be undergoing treatment for the next couple of months," Robert scolded.

"The doctor said the cancer has not spread, so it will be removed, and I should be back to normal in a few months. All I need is support from my loved ones," Leah said tenderly, looking at Robert.

Gwen made a puking sound that had Robert hurrying over to her side with worry. "Are you okay?"

"I just need a glass of water," Gwen said. He looked at the glass of water next to her. "With lime," she added, making a face.

"I'll be back." Robert exited, leaving the ladies alone. "So, you're dying," Gwen sneered.

"I'm not dying. The doctors say I'm going to live," Leah defended. "You never know what may happen. Enjoy yourself—your last day might just be drawing nearer," Gwen said. A chill went through her at the smile that engulfed Leah's face.

"I don't think so, dear. I don't think so."

She wondered what the woman meant as Leah walked away with more strength than the slow pace she had when she arrived with Robert. Gwen reflected on what Blake had told her—to be wary of Leah. Could Leah go to the lengths of pretending she had cancer? She didn't think the woman was that conniving.

Whatever the case, Leah would never have any power over her. Gwen was going to put her in her place like always. She was Robert's wife, and she would give him a family. Leah, on the other hand, was dying and would soon be out of their lives. However, Gwen would keep her memory, telling her children bedtime stories of a monster called Leah. She laughed heartily at the beautiful idea.

DANIELLE

"Is everything okay?" Brad asked. He stood in the mirror, putting on his tie. Danielle was on the bed, watching him.

"What do you mean?" she asked.

"I sense some reservation from you. You've been quiet these past few days."

Oh, so he had noticed. She had tried to act like things were okay, but how could she? She had to sleep next to him. She had to eat next to him. How could she hide the resentment she felt for him? Worse, she was scared to confront him. She feared what he would say to her. Would he lie to her and make her feel worse than she already felt?

"No, it's just… it is Gabby, my friend," Danielle said. "Are you referring to Dave's wife?"

"Exactly. You must have heard that Diana is back with a son. This is really a burden on Gabby, having some woman show up out of nowhere. I can't even imagine it happening to me. I would go crazy."

"You would?" Brad said quietly.

"Very. I don't even want to imagine myself in her shoes. It's not something I would take lightly."

"Remember, the child was before Gabby came into the picture." "That's true. Now, if he cheated and had the child during the marriage, that would make any woman crazy, don't you think?" Brad chuckled, but his eyes reflected no humor. "I guess so. Well, I must go. I won't be home for dinner. I have a business meeting with some clients."

She didn't even know if he was lying or being truthful anymore. In the days after she'd overheard him talking to his mistress, her mind had been in turmoil as she attempted to dissect if every meeting or trip he had taken or gone to had been an excuse to be with the other woman.

Danielle got off the bed. Standing in front of him, she straightened his tie. He kissed her, but she felt none of the sparks she used to feel.

As she settled back into her bed, she wondered if her feelings for her husband were fading away. Did she still love him? Yes, however, there had been a shift. She had always looked to Brad as her savior in some sort of way. She'd been submissive to him in every regard. In her eyes, Brad was perfect, and he made no mistakes. She'd believed Brad did what was right, and she couldn't question him. But now, Danielle saw him as the asshole she had trusted, and he had broken that trust. He was no longer on the pedestal she had once placed him on. With this revelation came doubts and questions. She was beginning to question herself and how much power she had given to her husband.

He didn't deserve her trust. She knew she couldn't keep up with the pretense for much longer. Her respect for him was beginning to fade, and everything about him had started to irk her. For example, just the other day at dinner, she had noticed how crooked his nose was. Last night, while they had sex, she had giggled, resisting a burst of full-fledged laughter at how his ridiculous sounds resembled that of a cow. She tried hard these days not to flare up and tell him to shut up when he said something stupid. One of these days, she might be unable to control herself and end up yelling at him.

It was time for her to change the tempo of her life. She grabbed her phone and scrolled through her contacts. Gwen had supplied her with the number of a discrete private investigator. Danielle didn't know what she would do with the information he would find, but she knew she needed it to confirm the suspicions and rumors.

She dialed the number, and a man with a gruff voice answered. She asked him a few questions to learn: Yes, he was the private investigator. Yes, he was available for her services. And yes, he was willing to meet this afternoon.

She hung up and lay on the bed, her heart racing with excitement.

CHAPTER EIGHT

TRINA & GABBY

"I think I should get a license to be a PI," Trina said. She had spent the last few days finding information on Diana.

And damn, it had not been easy. The woman had lived a quiet life prior to returning to Michigan. Trina had informed the women seated around the table that Diana lived in a townhouse owned in her name in London, and she worked on a charity board. She had a few friends she socialized with. "However, what I find very strange is that her son was never in any of her pictures. It's almost like she doesn't have a child. Like no mention of him at all. Nothing."

"Some parents don't like their children on social media," Danielle pointed out.

That was true. But this rubbed Trina the wrong way. It seemed like a deliberate attempt to hide him.

"The internet is a small place; maybe she didn't want Dave to know he had a son," said Gabby.

"That's true again, but I still insist that this is weird. Very weird. I mean, not even a picture or a mention of his name. I went through all 300 pictures of her on Instagram, and there was nothing about a son. It seems like too much trouble to hide the boy for so long and then reemerge with him."

The woman was certainly up to no good.

"You can always ask her," Gwen said with an eye roll. "Has Dave taken a DNA test?" Trina asked.

"What? That boy is Dave's son. There's no question about his paternity. He's his replica," Gabby said.

"Oh please, I've seen children who look a lot like their parents who turn out not to be their biological children," Trina said. Physical resemblance was not proof of a blood relationship. She had seen situations where a DNA test proved that.

"Gabby is right. That kid looked exactly like Dave when he was a boy. The child is his, and I think Dave would be insulted if Gabby asked for one," Danielle said.

"I don't want to do anything to upset Diana either. That woman's being a bitch!" Gabby said. "She's doing everything she can to make Dave miserable, and he's pulling away from me. Yesterday, he went to the hotel to spend some time with his son. The man hasn't seen his son in ten years, and she tells him he only has ten minutes?"

Diana was making him beg for his son. She was pushing him into a tight corner, and with Dave's feelings for her, he might bend to Diana's manipulation, which meant doom for Gabby.

"He barely says anything. He just mopes around," Gabby said, more to herself.

"Gabby, now is not the time to be defeated. You're letting Diana win by being weak. This is exactly what the woman wants, for you to lower your guard and allow her to walk right in and take control. Secure your marriage. Make your husband know you're going to be by his side. She wants war; let's give her war," Trina advised. She knew it wasn't easy, but her friend needed to be pushed.

When Trina returned home, Charles was at her door with flowers and a box of chocolate.

"Hey," he said, kissing her. "What are you doing here?"

"So, I have to call first?" He lifted a brow.

"I just wasn't expecting you," Trina admitted as they walked through the front door. He'd been more of a stranger, and with her busy work and friends' issues, she barely had time for him and his mother. In summary, there were more important things.

"I'm sorry," he said, his arms around her waist as he pulled her to him.

"For what?"

"I know I've been an asshole these past few weeks, and I promise to make up for it."

"Okay." She shrugged as she pulled away from him. "That's it?"

"What do you mean?"

"You were supposed to apologize too." Charles frowned. "For what?"

"You flirted with my cousin all through the party at my

parents' house!"

Oh. So, Charles had been mad at Trina because of that. Was he serious? "First of all, I didn't flirt with Denzel. We talked. And the only reason we kept each other company was because you neglected me."

"I did not neglect you."

"Really? I follow you to your mama's house, where I don't know anyone, and you leave me alone. Just like that. Is there another definition of neglect?" Trina threw at him.

"I hadn't seen Michelle in a long while."

"And I hadn't seen Denzel in a long while either. What did you expect me to do? Sit by your side and sing kumbaya?" "I was just—"

"No, Charles. I felt disrespected by your little friend and your mother." His eyes lit up, and she continued. "Yes, your mother. I could see right through her little act of pushing Michelle at you and treating me like trash. And I refuse to be treated that way by anyone!" Charles sighed, running his fingers through his locks. "I didn't know you were angry. I'm sorry, Trina. I didn't see things that way.

All I saw were you and Denzel talking and laughing, and my mom suggested that you two had…."

"Denzel asked me out in college, but I turned him down. He's a cool guy, but that's it. And even if something had happened, that was in the past. If he hadn't kept me company, I would've left your ass; I bet you that."

"I messed up big-time. Forgive me?" Charles asked with a grin. "Fine. But you have a lot to make up for. I'm going to pick an expensive restaurant and am very hungry." Charles chuckled. "I'm up for anything."

As they kissed, she remembered that he had not cleared up the issue with his mom and Michelle. He was trying to play it slick, and it wouldn't turn out in his favor.

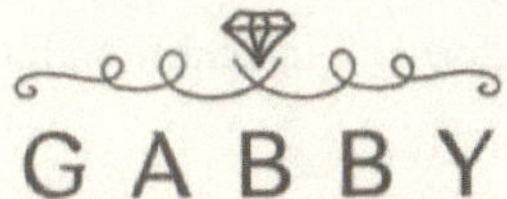

G A B B Y

The black car parked out front signaled to Gabby that her father-in- law was around, which was a rare occurrence. As much as Dave respected his parents, he had a distant relationship with his father and was closer to his mother. Growing up, his parents had always been too busy, and an army of nannies had raised him.

She handed the shopping bags to one of the maids. She is doing a lot of shopping nowadays. It was therapy to take her mind off all that was going on. However, it only worked at the moment. Once she was out of the shops, her reality was glaring her in the face.

Clifford Dodd once had a robust build, but the aftermath of a heart attack and a near stroke greatly affected his health. His new diet had made him lean, and he now used a cane after an injury he suffered during the heart attack. However, Clifford remained a powerful man and still dabbled in politics.

He was coming out of the library wearing a frown. It slipped away when he spotted her.

"Gabby, you're as beautiful as always," Clifford said as she leaned forward in a hug. He had been very accepting of her, despite her background. One would expect such a man with a respectful background wouldn't want her to be a part of his family. It had been Dave's mother who had been cold toward her at first; however, the woman was now polite to her.

"Are you staying for dinner?" she asked.

"No, I'm leaving now. I just came to have a talk with Dave about the boy."

Her mood turned sour. Did she have to be reminded of Diana and her son?

"I must leave now," Clifford said and headed for the door.

Dave sat at his desk, a glass of whiskey in hand. He looked tired. "What did Dad want to talk about?" she asked, closing the study door.

"He wants me to pay Diana off and send her away." Her eyes widened in surprise. "He said that?"

"Yes. We argued. If you had arrived two minutes sooner, you would've heard us yelling at each other," Dave said with a weak chuckle.

"Why does he want that?" Gabby wondered aloud.

"He believes having her around would disrupt things for me. In his words, I have a family now. If my son has been kept away for ten years and I have fared well, then I shouldn't be concerned about him now."

That was cold coming from Clifford. But she was comforted by his support for her. "I thought he adored Diana."

"I thought he did too. They were quite close, like father and daughter. But he won't make me change my mind. I'm not going to be cold and selfish like he was. My son is not going to have a distant father."

"Why did you cheat on Diana?" The question came out before she could stop herself.

Dave froze in surprise at the question. He was quiet for a while, and she decided he wouldn't answer her. But then, he began to speak. "Everyone said we were a perfect couple. We started dating in college, and marriage seemed inevitable. I loved her, you know. A lot. But..." He took a sip from his glass. "There was just something wrong with us. Diana was sweet, but at some point, she changed. It was like I was seeing different sides of her when other people were around. I could sense her holding back. She had secrets she refused to share with me. She could smile one moment and be so angry the next. And yes, vain. She wanted to be the center of attention, and you know me."

Yes, Dave was more of an introvert. He tended to surround himself with loudmouthed people, but he was quiet. The only reason he socialized was because of business.

He sighed. "You know, I don't even know how to explain it. Everything seemed good, but something was missing. It was like a vacuum, and it kept widening with every day that went bad. I think I was too much of a coward to end things between us. I knew if I sat her down, we would talk and end up back together, but I wanted out."

"So, you cheated on her."

Dave nodded. "And I let her know." He chuckled. "You know, she was stunned I would do such a thing. She... she always had... she had always worshipped, umm—she chose me. You know?"

Now he was babbling, obviously drunk. He grabbed the bottle and refilled his glass. She'd never seen him this way—tired and frustrated. She took the bottle and glass from him and, despite his protest, led him to their room.

He was still rambling as she took his shoes off and covered him with a blanket. In seconds, he was fast asleep.

How long would this continue with the both of them being miserable? The person benefiting from all this was Diana with her twisted goal. Gabby glanced at her sleeping husband. She wasn't going to lose him. No matter whatever Diana brought to the battlefield, Gabby was going to get more ammunition. She was softhearted, but there was a steely side to her that Diana would wish she hadn't tampered with.

CHAPTER NINE

TRINA

Trina had a visitor, one she was surprised to receive. Although she had exchanged numbers with Denzel weeks back, they hadn't spoken since. And now he was in her boutique, looking through a clothes rack.

"Need something for your woman?" she asked.

He turned around, and she couldn't help but marvel at how hot he really was. Charles was good-looking, but Denzel was fine as hell! She noticed the looks thrown his way by several women. Her assistant had been all smiles when she came to tell her someone wanted to see her.

"You've made a great place for yourself," Denzel commented. "Thank you. So, what do you want, Denzel?" she asked, getting straight to the point. She doubted this was a social visit.

He touched his chest like he was wounded. "You hurt me, Trina.

Can't I drop by to say hi to a friend?"

She scoffed. A friend indeed. They were more of acquaintances.

She doubted they had enough interaction to qualify as friends. "Are you free for lunch?" he asked, glancing at his Rolex.

Her stomach rumbled at the mention of food. She'd been busy all day. There had been a mix-up with a shipment, and handling it had stressed her. "There's a cafe a few blocks away. Let me get my purse." They walked to the small cafe she usually got a quick bite from.

When they entered, they noticed a vacant booth near the back. The waitress exchanged small talk with Trina before taking their orders.

"So, what do you want to talk about?" Trina asked, turning her attention to her guest.

"Always abrupt, Trina." Denzel grinned. "My aunt wants me to talk to you."

"And you agreed?"

"It came with an offer. She's going to push some money my way if I tell you to end things with Charles."

"You do know I'm not going to do that, right?"

"I know, but I had to try. Look, Trina, you know I support you every time. You're a strong and independent black woman. And you deserve a good man. But Charles is not the one for you, and you know it. His mother will always interfere in his life, and he will never stand up to her. It's always been that way. She has dictated almost everything he has done since he was born. All the ladies he had dated, she's scrutinized them, and if she didn't like them, he'd dump them. You're the only one he's dated without her approval."

"That should mean something, right?"

"What it means is that she's more than determined to get you out of the picture, Trina. When her family is threatened, which she believes is happening, she will do anything to bring down the threat. I've seen her destroy people just to show control. One time, one of her daughters' husbands was having an affair with a chick. She got the lady deported back to whatever country she came from. Brenda doesn't play fair."

Trina sighed. She didn't need any of these headaches in her life.

As much as she loved putting people in their place, she had a lot to contend with. Charles wasn't worth the drama, to be honest. However, she wasn't scared of Brenda.

"I appreciate your concern, Denzel, but Brenda owes me an apology for her skanky attitude. She needs to realize that I'm not a child that she can manipulate and treat like trash. Charles and I are just dating. It's nothing serious. I don't want her surname. She needs to chill," Trina said, already feeling a headache building.

"This might just be a fling to you, but to Charles, this is much more. I know my cousin, and he's crazy over you. You're different from the prim and proper women he's used to. You're a breath of fresh air and easy to fall for. I've spoken to him, and this is serious for him."

Denzel was right in that aspect. Perhaps she was hesitant to let go of Charles because she didn't want to hurt him. He had told her he loved her one night while she pretended to be asleep. Despite the whole macho look he portrayed, he was a softy. Her ending things with him would break his heart, and she didn't want that on her conscience.

"Like I said, the relationship will run its course, and Brenda can have her son marry who the hell she wants. I mind my own business, and I don't want any trouble, so she should let me be. Now can we enjoy our lunch?"

"So, in other words, you're not going to end things with him?" Trina didn't reply.

She left work a couple of hours later to meet up with her friends at the restaurant they had turned into one of their spots. Danielle was early as always, and Gwen arrived a few minutes later with shopping bags filled with clothes for her baby. Gabby was running late as usual. "She said she will be here soon," Danielle said, reading Gabby's text.

They were done with a bottle of wine when Gabby arrived. "I'm so sorry. I had lunch with Dave's mother," she said as she settled down.

"What did she want?" Trina asked.

"Moira wanted me to talk Dave into sending Diana and her son away," Gabby said.

"Was that not the same thing his father said a few days ago?" Danielle asked.

"Yes. She believes I can make Dave see reason, that having Diana and Adrian around is no good."

"And what reason is that?" Trina asked with interest.

"That Dave might decide to get into politics, and Diana would be a hindrance. I don't know, but that sounded like an excuse, and she sounded desperate. I have no idea why they wouldn't want their grandson around them." Gabby poured a healthy amount of wine into a glass.

It just didn't make sense that Dave's parents didn't want Diana around. Times had changed, and the political scene was more accepting of outside relations. This case was understandable because the child had been conceived before Dave's marriage. Why were his parents so adamant about Diana not being around? Unless....

"Hey! Watch it!" Gwen snapped as her wine sloshed from her glass after Trina bumped her arm.

"Sorry," Trina said as she regained her composure. "I have a crazy theory but hear me out."

"Shoot."

"What if Dave is not the father?" Trina asked. "I've told you the boy is—"

"What if the boy is Dave's brother?"

"Are you drunk? How can he be...." Gwen's eyes widened in understanding. "Wait, are you trying to say...?" Her face scrunched up in disgust.

"No way! You are out of your mind, Trina!

Gabby shook her head. "That can't be, Trina. Trash that thought. There's no way Clifford and Diana would ever.... Ewww! He's old enough to be her father. Why would she screw around with the father when the son is more than enough?"

Trina shrugged. "My idea is not far-fetched. We should know by now that the craziest things happen. Who knows if she likes them old? Look, we live in a messed-up world. It makes sense that way. Why would Diana up and leave such a fruitful relationship without forgiving Dave? Why did she go years without telling Dave about his son? Now, I don't know her clear intentions for returning, but it makes sense why Dave's parents don't want her around."

"So, you think Moira is in on it?" Danielle asked.

Trina nodded. "Old couples have a way of sticking together.

When exactly did Clifford have that heart attack?" "Ummm…." Gabby tried to remember.

"It was a few days before Diana left," Gwen said, staring at the bottle of wine.

"And you think that's a coincidence? Shit like that doesn't happen.

Everything is connected," Trina said, her heart racing in excitement. "I don't want to believe it. I don't." Gabby shook her head.

"It's not up to you to believe it, Gabby. There's only one way we can find out if Clifford is the boy's father."

"And that is?" Gabby asked.

"A DNA test. Between Clifford and Adrian."

Gwen chuckled. "Diana will never submit her son to such a test. It's an insult to her. And Clifford? We're talking about a retired mayor. To even suggest such a thing is a scandal."

"Gwen is right. The parties are never going to agree to it. It's a huge insult that will only make Diana up and leave," Danielle agreed.

"Who even mentioned having their consent?" Trina smiled.

Understanding dawned amongst her friends. "How are we going to do it?" Gabby asked.

Trina was glad her friend wasn't talking about how crazy the assumption was any longer.

"The way we always do things. We plan, and then we strike."

CHAPTER TEN

GABBY & TRINA

Three days later, Gabby entered Moira and Clifford's kitchen while they were enjoying breakfast. Moira's face said it all; she was surprised to see her. Gabby had timed her entrance perfectly.

"Gabby! Is everything okay?" Moira asked as she kissed her cheeks. Clifford curiously looked on.

"I'm sorry I didn't call ahead. I just… I can't get through to Dave," she said, wearing a sad look.

The expression that passed Moira's face made Gabby lean toward Trina's theory. Dave's parents were more concerned with the matter than they ought to be.

"What did he say?" Moira asked as she signaled at the butler to get an extra serving for Gabby.

"He's been talking to Drew. With the child having Diana's name, it will be difficult to fight for custody. He believes an arrangement with Diana is going to work best. But Diana is being stubborn. I suspect she has ulterior motives for returning." Gabby took a sip of the tea in front of her.

"What motives?" Clifford asked.

"I don't know. I haven't told Dave, but she threatened me that she would destroy our marriage." Her voice quaked as she relived the horrible experience.

"She said that?" Moira asked, anger sparking in her eyes. "Yes." Gabby nodded as she patted her lips with a napkin.

"I apologize for that, Gabby. Do you see why we've been insisting that Dave pay her off? She's trouble for us, and we must unite to get her out of our lives," Moira said in a steely voice.

"I agree." Gabby nodded before sneezing into her napkin. "Excuse me. I need to freshen up."

Dave's parents leaned into a conversation as she walked into the hallway. There was a powder room by the foyer, but she ignored it. She made her way upstairs, her heart racing. She was familiar with the staff, but it might seem odd to have her roaming about. She went down the hallway to the room occupied by Clifford. Dave had given her a tour of the house on the first day he brought her to meet his parents. He had let it slip once that his parents slept in separate rooms.

She sighed in relief as the door opened, and she peeked in. No one was inside. She headed straight for the vanity table. Bottles of body products lined the table, but that wasn't what she needed. Her eyes quickly spotted a comb. It was filled with white hair, which she identified as Clifford's. She pulled the plastic bag out of her pocket and placed some strands in it. Afterward, she hurried to the door and made her way downstairs.

When she joined them, the couple pulled away from their conversation.

"I'm sorry, I cannot stay any longer. I just got a phone call, and I need to attend to some matters," Gabby said with a sweet smile.

"We have to talk during the week about this problem," Moira said as she saw her to the door.

"Yes, we do," Gabby agreed. She could feel the woman's gaze as she got into the car. The moment she drove out of her in-law's compound, she called the others.

"I'm on my way," she said.

Gabby met the other ladies at a small restaurant near the S Hotel. They were rounding up their breakfast. With Gwen concentrating on her third croissant, she didn't even acknowledge Gabby.

"Did you get it?" Danielle asked.

She slid the plastic bag across to Danielle.

"So, we move on to the next phase," Trina said.

The next phase took place at the S Hotel. Gwen grumbled the entire short ride over there that she had better things to do, but the others ignored her. Danielle drove and slid into an empty parking spot with a view of the entrance.

"We know what has to be done," Trina said. Everyone nodded. The plan was simple: get the DNA of Clifford and Adrian. They had gotten Clifford's, and now it was on to Adrian's. It was going to be a challenge with Diana in the picture. She wasn't someone to be easily fooled.

Gabby watched as Trina got out of the car and headed straight for the hotel lobby. They could hear her footsteps through the headphones they had plugged in.

No one stopped Trina as she made her way to the restroom. The shuffling sound they heard was her changing from her outfit into the cleaning staff's costume. Gwen had paid off one of the cleaning ladies the previous day to allow Trina to work one hour of her shift.

"I'm headed to the room, ladies. Now is the time," Trina said.

Gabby dialed Diana's number. She didn't answer until the second ring.

"Who's this?" she asked sweetly.

"Hello, Diana, this is Gabby. I want to talk to you."

"There's nothing to talk about," Diana said coldly.

"Please, Diana, spare me a few minutes of your time. I just want to talk to you about Dave and Adrian. I—"

"I have nothing to talk to you about."

Gabby glared at the phone as the call ended. At least they had tried. There had always been the possibility of Diana refusing to see her. Now it was up to Trina to go ahead with the plan.

Gabby took a deep breath. She hoped the plan wasn't going to flop. Her marriage depended on this plan being a success.

TRINA

Trina took one step at a time, pushing the cleaning supplies trolley. She hated the starchy outfit she had on. It was so freaking tight and reeked of bleach. The things she did for friends. However, she knew she could count on them if she were in a mess.

No one paid her any attention; the help was usually ignored. She stopped in front of Diana's room and knocked on the door. With how long it took for the woman to open up, Trina wondered if Diana was inside.

"You're late!" Diana snapped as she flung the door open.

The woman was beautiful; she had to give her that. With smooth skin and what would be termed an aristocratic nose, she was one of those women who men wanted as a trophy. However, Trina wasn't one to be deceived by a pretty face. If she was right, then Diana was an ugly person behind her physical appearance.

"I need my room cleaned. I saw a cobweb this morning. I don't know if you're blind or something. Change the sheets too. I need this room cleaned. Understand?" Diana rattled on.

"Yes," Trina said.

The living quarter was a suite, and as the maid had informed Gwen, it contained a living room, a bedroom, a bathroom, and a kitchenette, which most of the occupants never used.

Her eyes rested on a boy who sat on the couch, his eyes glued to the TV. Well, he did look like Dave, with those pointed ears and dark eyes, which must have made Diana's plan easy. If Adrian were a toddler, it would've been a breeze getting what Diana wanted from him. But kids this age were smart and couldn't be easily manipulated.

"Start with the room!" Diana snapped.

Trina hated house chores. Gabby was making her do crazy shit today. She headed to the bedroom and stared in disgust at the room. Couldn't Diana at least make the bed? The room was messy, with empty pizza boxes and trash lying about.

"Gabby, you're going to get me a Dior bag, I swear," Trina mumbled into the earphone, rolling her eyes at the chuckle that came from the other side.

Trina worked slowly, first attending to the bed. "What is she doing here?" Gabby hissed.

"Who?" Trina mumbled as Diana walked in, and Trina looked downward. Diana had never seen her, but she didn't want to be easily recognized elsewhere. How was she supposed to get Adrian alone?

"Be fast! I haven't got all—" Diana began before being interrupted by a knock on the door. Diana went to it, and Trina heard a female voice.

"Trina, my mother-in-law, is there," Gabby said.

"I think she's the one who just walked in," Trina whispered. She glanced out of the room and saw an older woman with Diana. The woman glared at Diana with anger.

"Take the boy somewhere," the woman said. "I—"

They both turned to Trina when she stepped into the room. She had never met Moira, so she doubted the woman knew her.

"You! Take the boy for a ten-minute walk," Moira instructed.

Trina bit back the urge to snap at her that she wasn't a nanny, but this was the opportunity she had been looking for.

"Umm…." Trina looked at the boy, who hesitated.

"Adrian, follow the woman. Don't get too close to her; you don't want to catch anything. And you better take good care of my son," Diana warned.

Up close, the boy was such a cutie, and Trina felt her ovaries squeeze in desire for one of her own. His little hand slid into hers as they headed out.

As the door closed behind them, she wished she could be a fly in the room. She should've left her earphones there, but she needed to keep tabs with the other ladies.

"Who's that woman?" Adrian asked in a sweet voice.

"Your… I don't know," Trina corrected herself before telling the boy it was probably his stepmother. "Hey, why don't I show you a trick?"

A smile spread on his face at the suggestion.

They were now downstairs by the elevator. Trina didn't want to wander around and get unwarranted attention that would expose her.

"Close your eyes," Trina said.

The boy closed his eyes. She reached behind him and cut a few strands of hair with the scissors she had in her apron. She quickly placed them in the plastic bag and returned it to her apron, bringing out a piece of candy she had brought along on a whim.

"Magic!" she said when the boy opened his eyes.

He looked disappointed. "Mommy said I shouldn't eat candy."

The elevator door opened, and Moira stormed out, wearing a pleasing look. That had been over quickly.

Trina held back a gasp when they returned to the room. There was a bruise on Diana's face that had not been there when she left. Moira had sure done a number on her.

"Mommy, what happened to you?" Adrian asked, concerned as he hugged his mother.

"Mommy ran into the wall." Diana smiled as she ran her fingers through the boy's hair.

Trina headed back to the bedroom to grab her cleaning supplies. Heck, she wasn't going to continue cleaning this freaking room. She had gotten what she wanted, and as she exited the bedroom, she heard Diana on the phone.

"Hey, I need you to get us two plane tickets. Yes. Adrian and I will be leaving on Friday. Yes."

Diana was leaving the country so soon. That was quite interesting. She turned her attention to the broom as she heard approaching footsteps.

"You, come back later," Diana snapped. "I—"

"Later!"

Trina was more than happy to oblige. She placed the supplies in the trolley and headed out. She went into the restroom she had switched clothes in earlier and changed back into her clothes. Then, she hurried out into the parking lot.

The moment the car door closed, Trina shoved the plastic bag at Gabby. "Like you heard, Diana is leaving by this weekend."

"Seems like she's running away," Gwen said.

"There was a bruise on her face. Your mother-in-law probably hit her. And I noticed a broken vase. It wasn't there when I left," Trina informed.

"Moira must have threatened her," Gabby said.

"Or paid her off. Or both. I'm pretty sure she's aware the child is her husband's," Trina said.

"We don't even know if that's true," Gabby countered.

Trina scoffed. "How else can you explain what just happened? Man cheats with a younger woman dating his son, she gets pregnant, and he has no option but to tell his wife. They pay her off, and she leaves the country. She's probably run out of money and returned to cause trouble and get more money. You need to get a DNA test as soon as possible."

"If she leaves, that's good for you. Your troubles are solved," Gwen said.

"No," Gabby disagreed. "Dave will continue to think the child is his. He'll hate himself, and probably me, for not having the opportunity to be with his child. He needs to know the truth."

"Well, I know someone who can have it tested and have the results back by Friday," Gwen said.

"I hope we're not too late," Danielle said.

CHAPTER ELEVEN

GABBY & TRINA

The past three days had been a long wait for Gabby. What usually took weeks had set her back a few thousand dollars to have done in days, but it was worth it. As much as she wanted Diana out of her life, she didn't want a broken marriage, which was bound to happen.

"What does it say?" Gwen snapped.

The four ladies were in the clinic lobby where the test had been done. Days before, Gabby had presented three labeled DNA specimens from Clifford, Dave, and Adrian to the lab technician.

"Clifford is the father," Gabby said.

Sighs of relief fell amongst her friends, but she was the most relieved. Dave wasn't the father! Thank goodness. Now she wouldn't have to contend with Diana. The woman had been exposed for the wretch that she was. It was ironic that, despite the so-called respected family and background Diana had come from, she had turned out to be a horrible manipulator. With her poor upbringing, Gabby would never think of doing such a thing.

Gwen's phone rang, and she frowned as she stared at the screen.

"It's the maid from the hotel." Gwen had given her money to act as a spy to inform them when Diana was leaving the country. "Hello? Right now? Okay." "Diana has her suitcases set and should be leaving in a few minutes."

Damn! "I need to get to Dave right now!" Otherwise, Diana would slip away, and they might never be able to confront her.

"You might be too late," Danielle said.

"Don't worry, go get Dave. I'll distract her," Gwen said with a coy smile as she patted her stomach.

Despite how tense the situation was, Gabby couldn't help but smile. Gwen was just the drama they needed to stall the other woman. "We'll head to the hotel, and you can meet us there. Is that okay with you?" Trina asked.

Gabby nodded. She hurried out of the clinic with the test results in her bag. With how fast she drove, it was a wonder the cops didn't pull her over. In a few minutes, she had pulled into the parking lot of Dave's office. She half ran through the lobby and got on the elevator.

Usually, she stopped and chatted with a couple of Dave's employees. But not today.

"Mrs.—"

Gabby waved away the secretary as she burst through the door of Dave's office. The five men who were having a meeting all turned to her in surprise.

"Gabby? What's wrong?" Dave asked, concerned.

"I'm sorry for interrupting your meeting, but I need to talk to you. Now!"

Hearing the urgency in her voice, Dave turned to the gentlemen and said, "I'm really sorry, but this is an emergency. Can we reschedule?"

"Tomorrow then," one of the men said with a glare at her.

"What is so important that you had to disrupt such an important meeting? We were about to close a deal, Gabby!" Dave scolded in annoyance.

"Adrian is not your son!" Gabby spat out.

Dave froze. Then his eyes shone with fury. "Seriously, Gabby? Look, it's hard enough dealing with Diana. I don't need any of this right now."

She placed the envelope on his table. He looked at it warily. "What is that?"

"A DNA test. You are not his father."

He quickly removed the paper from the envelope and unfolded it. His eyes widened as he read the results. "Adrian is my brother? Are you fucking with me?" he yelled.

She took a step backward. She had never seen him this mad. "Fuck!" he yelled as he tossed the items off his table. She hurried over to him and placed her hands on his shoulders. "I'm so sorry, Dave. I'm sorry."

"I…. When…. How? Is this possible?"

"We… I had my suspicions. I really don't know the details, but you can get them from Diana. But we need to get there now. She's leaving the country in a few minutes with the boy."

His body tensed at this. He was pissed. "Let's go," he said, grabbing his keys.

The ride to the hotel was quiet. She could feel him fuming. And his reaction was well deserved. His father and girlfriend had messed around, and then the woman had tried to pin a child on him. How cruel could one be?

Gabby's eyes were on her phone as she interacted with Danielle, who was listening in on Diana and Gwen from the parking lot. From what Gabby understood, Trina had an emergency and rushed off after dropping Gwen off at the hotel.

From what Danielle could gather from Gwen and Diana's conversation, Gwen had pretended to bump right into her in the halls. With a little convincing, Diana let her into her room to use the bathroom. Danielle was sure Gwen mentioned that the baby had been sitting on her bladder all day.

So far, Gwen was delaying her by making small talk about Robert allowing Leah to be in his life, but it seemed Diana didn't have time for her drama. She had already called a cab.

A few minutes later, Gabby tried to keep up with Dave's long strides as he hurried toward the elevator. He wore a pensive look like he was headed for war.

The door to Diana's room flung open before he could reach for the handle. Diana turned pale at the sight of him, and her eyes shot to Gabby.

"Wh-What are you doing here, Dave?" she asked, putting on a fake smile.

"Where's the boy?" Dave asked in a steely voice. "He's… he's in the room," Diana said.

"Gwen, take the boy downstairs," Dave ordered.

Usually, Gwen would've mouthed off, but she did as she was told.

She went into the bedroom and returned with a confused Adrian. "Go with her. Mommy will be with you soon," Diana said.

As the door closed behind them, Gabby's heart ached for the boy.

He was innocent and shouldn't have been used by his mother. "Dave, you're not going to intimidate me into staying. I gave you

an ultimatum—choose your son and me or her." Diana pointed at Gabby.

Gabby went still. Really? The nerve of her!

"Cut the bullshit! I know Adrian's not my son. I know you slept with my father!" Dave yelled.

Diana's eyes widened. Then she burst into tears. "He… he raped me," she sobbed as she collapsed on a couch.

Had Clifford raped her? Gabby couldn't reconcile with the man she knew doing such a horrible thing. But then…

"I've had enough of you and your lies!" Dave said as he took a step forward.

Just as quickly as the tears had come, they disappeared. Gabby resisted the urge to applaud her acting. The woman was good.

"Fine! Do you want to hear the truth? Your father and I were having an affair. Are you happy now? Are you?" Diana yelled.

The beautiful woman had transformed into a monster, and Gabby had never been as disgusted by anyone as she was by

Diana. Nothing justified what Diana had done to Dave.

Dave looked defeated. "I loved you. I cared for you, and of all men, my father?"

"Love wasn't enough! I had bills to pay. My family was in debt, and you refused to give me the life I wanted. Your father was there for me! He gave me all I wanted instead of giving me the bullshit 'love' you always talked about!"

"You made me hate myself for cheating on you; meanwhile, you were with my father. To you, I was just a fool," Dave said.

"Look, I did love you at some point. But like I said, love wasn't enough.

Your father pampered me. He took care of me," Diana continued.

"But he wasn't with you when you got pregnant? He left you hanging," Dave spat out.

Her face scrunched into a frown, and tears welled in her eyes as Dave continued. "Did you expect he would leave my mother for you? I guessed when he turned you away; you realized you were just like the other women before you."

"Don't!" she yelled. Then she took a deep breath. "You, your father, and your mother are all users! You used me as a pretty face and—"

"Don't turn this on us, Diana. You made your decision. You left when you realized there was nothing for you."

"Fine, I left. But your parents paid me off. They bought me a house, and I was to go far away," Diana said.

"And why did you return?" Gabby asked.

Diana shot her a look as if realizing she was there.

"The only reason she returned was because she ran out of money. How much did my parents give you this time around? Enough to have you gone for the next ten years, I suppose?" Dave sneered.

"You have no idea how difficult it is to raise a kid alone when all your friends are married to husbands who provide for them! So don't judge me!" Diana spat.

"I'm so glad that Adrian is not my son. To even think of having a child with a vile creature like you disgust me. I'm glad you left. You were the biggest mistake I ever made. Good luck with your life."

The door slammed hard as Dave stormed out. Gabby turned to Diana, seeing her for the miserable, broken woman she was. She'd had a pretty face and hadn't made the most of it. And now she should feel ashamed of her actions.

"Happy now? You can enjoy him for all I care. But I bet you, someday, your happiness will be destroyed."

Gabby chuckled. To think she had once felt threatened by her. "You are miserable, Diana. Damn miserable. I might have grown up in extreme poverty, but at least I'm not a miserable manipulator like you. In this game, you lost."

The woman burst into tears as Gabby left. She felt no pity for her. Dave was in the lobby talking to Gwen, his hand on the boy's shoulder. Gabby did feel pity for the boy, though. He was caught up in the lies and games of his parents and might suffer for it. "I should take the boy back to his mother," Gwen said.

"I'll talk to you later. I will text Trina and Danielle. I'm sure Danielle is tired of hanging out in the parking lot. We all can meet up tomorrow to talk. Thanks again, Gwen," Gabby mumbled to her friend.

As she reached for the car door handle, Dave pulled her to him, her head resting on his shoulder.

"I want you to know that I never would've left you. I love you too much to do that," Dave said.

Gabby smiled up at him. Hell yeah! She was never letting him go. "You ladies have missed all of the fireworks. Dave was pissed. Let's meet up for breakfast tomorrow. It's been a long day." Gabby texted.

"Sounds like a good plan," Danielle replied.

"You know, I was waiting to get a text so I could come and beat Diana's ass. All of this doesn't make any sense." Trina added.

"I'm headed home. Being pregnant sucks," Gwen said as she flagged down her driver.

TRINA

Trina hurried to the breakfast date with Gwen, Danielle, and Gabby. They had met this morning, and Gabby had given them a rundown of all that had happened since Trina had gotten a call on the way to the hotel to return to her store as soon as possible. After Trina had dropped off Gwen, she'd paid the clerk at the front desk to call Diana down to the desk for an urgent matter. Gwen had planned to bump into her as she returned to her room and invited herself in. Her plan worked like a charm. Diana hadn't expected anything.

Dave, on the other hand, had chosen not to confront his parents. However, he was pretty sure they knew he was aware of the truth. He was still pissed that they had gotten involved in such a mess, especially his father. Although Dave wanted nothing to do with Diana, he had a brother, and somehow, he was going to be there for him.

These rich folks had a lot going for them. *Lots of secrets and drama*, Trina couldn't help but think. It seemed the more money, the more skeletons in the closet.

She tucked all the problems into a corner of her mind as she pulled in front of her shop. Two weeks ago, one of her major designers stopped supplying her for no reason. She had discarded the move, not thinking much of it. But with what had happened now, she knew it had been an attack against her.

When Trina had rushed to her shop the other day, her assistant gave her a letter from a law firm. The building had been sold, and she had thirty days to move out, or her business would be shut down. She took a deep breath. The building was owned by an older man who had refused to sell the property for years. But when money exchanged hands, decisions tended to sway. Her business was situated in one of the best locations in town. Her clients had been coming here for the past three years. Getting a great location at an affordable rate was going to be hell.

This had been no ordinary sale. She knew who was behind it. Somehow Brenda had gotten through to her landlord and bought the building. Brenda was trying to destroy her. A cold smile spread on her face. If Brenda wanted war, she was going to get it.

ACT 2

DANIELLE'S NEMESIS

CHAPTER ONE

DANIELLE & TRINA

Danielle stared at the pictures the private investigator had given her of her husband in the arms of another woman— a woman she would never have thought him capable of mingling with. She was entirely different from her. She wore loud and tight clothes and was quite endowed in her bust and butt. With her colorful makeup, she looked nothing like the quiet and tamed woman Brad wanted Danielle to be.

There were pictures of him on dates in fancy restaurants with this woman on nights he had claimed to be working while she was home alone. Some shots showed them making out in the lobbies of hotels and various locations. There were even pictures of them in the woman's apartment. The PI had taken photos from the building across the street with a perfect view into her windows. These were the ones that infuriated her the most. These were images of them having sex. Her fingers clenched as she examined the proof in front of her.

Her husband was an asshole! Surprisingly, she hadn't done anything crazy since receiving the PI's evidence. She kept up with her smile; meanwhile, her eyes shot daggers and bullets at him. How could he act so shamelessly? He was a pretender who had perfected the act of being the dutiful husband with her, but out of her sight, he was a cheating scumbag.

Danielle studied the bank statements the PI had also given her. Her darling husband bankrolled this woman's lifestyle. He paid for her apartment, bought her a car, paid her credit cards off, and provided overseas trips.

And she wasn't the first. The investigator had found other women he had provided for in the past years. Although he wasn't still dating them, it was obvious the sort of relationship he'd had with them. Her husband was a serial cheater. She knew two of the women he had messed around with. One was an employee at the company, some girl named Jessica, who Danielle had bonded with at the company's yearly gala a few years back. She recalled Brad telling her not to get too close to Jessica because she had an unruly and wild character. Danielle hadn't noticed those traits in the girl, but she had listened to her husband. Now she knew better. He hadn't wanted her to be close to his past lover.

The other was a friend of his sister, Cindy, a model who wore skimpy clothes all over social media. She recalled Cindy having a fallout with her a while ago; she had inquired about what caused the conflict between the friends, but Cindy hadn't responded. It probably had to do with Brad. It was clear to her now that his family knew about his cheating ways. In all of this, Danielle had been foolish and the last to know—all because she had trusted her husband so much.

She took a deep breath. Seeing the truth didn't make her cry as she had thought it would. Instead, it gave her a calm sense of comfort by proving her suspicions weren't wrong.

And then, she looked at the last file provided by the PI. It was Brad's financial statements, both personal and that of the company, from before they got married. He had been in debt, and his father's company had been close to bankruptcy. He had married her for her money. Their marriage had restored him financially and saved his family's company with that merger with Danielle's parents.

Overall, the PI had done a great job—she had paid a lot for his discreet services. For over two months, he had followed Brad on his escapades out of town. The PI had also interviewed her husband's former lovers, giving Danielle all the ammunition she would need.

To be honest, she wasn't upset that Brad had married her for her money; after all, people married for many different reasons, not just love. But he had been fooling around and squandering her money on whores! He had spent a fortune in the past few years on these women while he gave her peanuts, making her feel like he was doing her a favor. It infuriated her.

Her money! On those women! She glared at the papers. She had been naïve and foolish for years, but not any longer. Now she saw her husband for the manipulative, cheating bastard he was.

The question was, what would she do with all this information? Was she going to pretend nothing had happened? Hell no! She was brimming with so much anger and disgust. The right thing to do was confront Brad, but she knew how things would go. He would apologize and promise never to do it again, but he might cheat on her anyway. Besides, she didn't trust him anymore with her body, heart, or money. It was time to take back the control she had never had.

Danielle kept the documents and pictures in a folder and returned them to her closet, where she knew he wouldn't find them. She had duplicated them, giving one to each of her friends for safekeeping. Like her, Gabby, Trina, and Gwen were pissed that Brad had been spending so much on his mistresses. This was money she would have put into charity or even invested in a business.

She stood in front of the mirror in her walk-in closet, staring at herself. She couldn't keep living this way—a wife to a cheating husband who had no respect and regard for her. It was a wonder he hadn't given her a disease, but he might one of these days. Or perhaps he had a child out there. It was time she protected herself in all ways. She had let Brad, as well as his family, control her life. Danielle had seen in the financial records the money that went to his family; that made her angry! And the nerve of them, taking her for a naïve woman.

She smiled. She was going to surprise them. She was going to show them that she wasn't someone they could step all over and treat like a cash cow. Brad had stepped on the tail of a sleeping serpent, and he was about to get bit.

Did she want to divorce Brad? She didn't have an answer to that. However, she knew she had enough evidence for walking away with a fortune, leaving him bleeding dry.

Grabbing her phone, she called her stylist and made an appointment within the hour. Then she called Julia. Julia Silva was her distant cousin. For a long time, she had heard her mother complain about how Julia was too independent and how being a lawyer ruined her life. She had no husband, and she had no children. All she had was a career. Her mother would rather have her married with several children.

"Danielle? It's a surprise to hear from you. Is everything okay?" Julia asked.

"I need your help. When will you be available?" "In a few hours."

That was enough time to finish her hair appointment and go shopping. They decided on a time and a restaurant before ending the call.

A couple of hours later, Danielle stared at herself in the mirror. Her once brown hair had been dyed blonde. It was a completely different look, making her cheekbones more pronounced and her eyes pop out. She loved the look!

Next, she headed to the mall to get some clothes, shoes, bags, and jewelry. She had to stop herself several times from buying the clothes she usually bought. Although she liked her style, she had always been tempted to try something else— tight-fitting clothes, prints, colors, metro—and this was her opportunity to do so. With some of the bags in her car and the others to be delivered to her home, she headed over to the restaurant for her appointment with her cousin.

"Danielle! You… you did something with your hair," Julia noticed as they hugged.

"I did."

"And it looks good on you," Julia said as a waiter poured them a glass of wine. "I must admit, I'm curious about your call. What can I do for you?"

With a cold smile, Danielle said, "I need your help to get control of my company."

TRINA

Brenda wore a frown as Trina opened the door with a smile. Trina didn't even attempt to tighten her lingerie robe, which left nothing to the imagination.

"Charles is not around. He went out to get us breakfast," Trina said, although she was pretty sure the woman was aware. She'd probably been parked outside, watching her son leave.

Pushing past her, Brenda made her way into the apartment, her eyes taking note of the changes Trina had made. She had gotten rid of the formal paintings, replacing them with colorful pieces by black artists.

"We need to talk, Trina," Brenda said.

"Oh, now you want to talk. You didn't want to talk a few months ago when you kicked me out of my building," Trina stated with her hands on her hips. She was out of business for weeks before she'd found another space to move to. And, heck, it had not been easy! Dave, Gabby's husband, had stepped in, and a friend of his had rented her a space in an even better location.

"I don't know what you're talking about," Brenda said innocently.

Trina laughed. *Yeah, right.* During the past two months, things had gotten serious with Charles. However, it was more on his part, and the thought of hurting him scared her. That man loved with all his heart! She did like him, but her feelings didn't amount to what he felt for her. To his mother's disgust, he'd started taking her to all family functions. Thank goodness he'd learned his lesson, and now he treats her with more respect than he did the first time she'd been a guest at a family event.

"What do you want, Brenda? Because there's nothing for us to talk about."

"Charles asked for his grandmother's ring."

Trina gasped. Hell no! She'd felt something was up with him. He'd been sneaky on his phone, and now it made sense; he was planning to ask her to marry him. Fucking hell! She hadn't signed up for this! Marriage? It was way too soon. What the hell was wrong with him?

"I see you're as repulsed as I am. I know you don't love my son," Brenda said.

"I never said that."

"You marrying him will be a mistake that will end with you hurting him. So please do the right thing and end this charade with him. Charles is not the man for you, and you're not the woman for him."

"You still got that nasty attitude of yours. You think you know what's best for your son, huh? Do you think you can control his life just like you control everyone else? Let me tell you some real shit. You're going to destroy your son's life! You're going to fucking push him away from you. He'll rebel someday, and you'll realize you no longer have control of him. It's just a matter of time."

Trina could tell her words hit hard as fear filled the woman's eyes for an instant. "I raised my son well, I did, and I'll do what's best for him."

Trina scoffed. "No, you do what's best for yourself. That's the only person you think of."

The door creaked, and the women hastily stepped away from each other as Charles walked in with a brown bag filled with their breakfast. He looked surprised at the sight of the two women together.

"Mom? What are you doing here this early?" Charles asked, giving Trina a worried look.

She smiled at him in return. "Is there a specific time range when I can check on my son? I was in the area, and I decided to drop by." "I'll go freshen up," Trina said before heading for the stairs,

feeling Charles's worried gaze on her.

She took a deep breath as she shut the bedroom door behind her. Why couldn't Charles take things slow with her? Couldn't they just date with no strings attached? He told her that his past relationships had always been calculated with the future in mind. She should have known this was how things were going to end.

Marriage? Most of her friends were married with children. She had been invited to more weddings than she could count in the last couple of years, and her social media timelines were flooded with wedding pictures and baby gender reveals. As much as Trina felt marriage wasn't her thing, every once in a while, she felt the urge to be with someone she could wake up with every morning—a husband. The idea of being married was tempting, to have a ring on her finger, but she worried it wasn't for her. She didn't have the patience to deal with a man who didn't have the balls to tell his mom to back off. Charles was thoughtful, caring, and generous, with many other attributes, but their chemistry would not sustain them in the long run.

She covered her face with her hands. She didn't want to end this, but she had to. He would be hurt, but so would she. Usually, she walked away without looking back, but Charles had touched a soft spot in her, though not enough to make her stay.

There was a knock on the door, and she regained her composure as Charles walked in. He watched her closely.

"Are you okay, Trina?"

"Sure am; why wouldn't I be?" She forced a smile.

He shrugged. "I don't know. It seemed like you were having a conversation with my mama when I walked in. Did she say anything to upset you?"

Trina laughed, brushing it off. "There's nothing to worry about. Your mama and I are cool." Seeing the disbelief in his eyes, she continued, "At least we try to be cool. I'm so hungry. Tell me you got those fried egg sandwiches and hashbrowns with sausage on the side 'cause I've been dreaming of them all week long."

And just like that, she'd distracted him; however, she was a bubbling mess inside.

CHAPTER TWO

GWEN & GABBY

If she heard that woman's voice one last time, Gwen was going to yell. It infuriated her. Her baby kicked, and she smiled. Her child agreed with her. It seemed every time Leah walked into the room, her baby moved. When this child was born, she was going to lay down some strict rules. Leah would never touch or see her child.

That was it! And nothing Robert said would change her mind.

Leah walked into the room with Robert's arm around her waist, helping her up. A teal scarf covered her bald head. Since starting the cancer treatments, she had gotten much thinner and now looked like a ghoul, which matched her true character.

Gwen shook her glass. "I need more orange juice."

It was annoying seeing Robert attend to someone other than her. His undivided attention was supposed to be on her. Damn Leah and her stupid cancer. Gwen's eyes narrowed on the other woman. Trina had said the timing was too suspicious, and she had to agree. Gwen got pregnant, and Leah got diagnosed with cancer. As much as the woman looked sick and underwent chemo treatments, Gwen still doubted her being ill. It was crazy for Leah to lie about something so serious, but she knew what people were capable of. And with what Blake, Leah's nephew, had hinted at, at how crazy Leah was, Gwen wouldn't put it past her. However, she couldn't tell her suspicions to Robert. He wouldn't believe her, especially when she had no evidence.

In an attempt to find proof, Gwen had gone into Leah's room when Leah wasn't around and checked her drug cabinet. The drugs in there were for cancer patients. She had also checked the test results, and they were legit. But still, she wasn't convinced. Leah looked weak, no doubt, but her eyes were calculating. Gwen could feel them on her, and they unnerved her more than she was ready to admit.

The baby moved again. Her due date was drawing near, and she wanted Leah out of the house before her baby was born. She had tried being civil with Robert, but the man was just too damn stubborn! He refused to move his best friend elsewhere. He was scared she would die, and he wanted to be around her.

However, Gwen would expose her if she were lying about her health. She had hired the services of the PI Danielle had used to find out about her husband's tacky affairs. Although Gwen knew he was a cheater, she had thought Brad had more class than to go for the women he fooled around with. But she shouldn't have been surprised; his father was known to pick up hookers off the street in the old days.

It was costly to retain the PI due to the nature of the situation; health records were difficult to secure because of privacy laws. But she was sure he would deliver, and then she would know the truth. If Leah was indeed sick, it was only a matter of time before she croaked. And if she were lying, she would be kicked out the door—the latter pleased Gwen more.

Robert returned with a pitcher full of orange juice, which he poured into her glass.

"How is the preparation for the baby shower going?" Robert asked.

He had given her quite a generous budget for the shower, and she was going to make the most of it, throwing an intimate but luxurious party. Not just anyone was going to be invited. The invitations had been sent, and the party would be held in a few weeks.

"Good, but I need more money; I need to get a cherub ice sculpture," Gwen said.

"I will have my assistant forward the money to you," Robert said. "Do I need an invite to attend?" Leah mumbled.

Leah's voice made Gwen wince. It was so bland and disguised in fake pain. Popping a cookie into her mouth, Gwen said, "No."

Robert frowned at this. "Why are you not having Leah over? She's a part of the family."

"She may be a part of your family but not mine. Even my cousins aren't going to be there. Only close friends and family will attend my shower, and Leah is neither of those. It's a shower, not a funeral. I don't want anyone to be depressed."

Gwen grabbed her juice-filled glass and staggered up, heading for her room. She was already feeling a headache from Leah's presence.

Just as expected, Robert followed her to the room, wearing an angry look. "I don't like the way you talk to Leah. I understand you've never been on good terms with her, but she's sick! Leah might die. Right now, she needs love and affection. She needs the will to survive, and you're not helping by antagonizing her."

Hands on her hips, Gwen glared at her husband. "You promised me I wouldn't have any problems, but Leah is a major problem. I don't like having her around!"

"Leah is my ex-wife and has been my friend for years!"

"I don't care! I don't like her. I don't want her here. I don't care if she has one foot in the grave. Her presence makes me uncomfortable. Every time she walks into the room, my baby gets upset. You need to make a decision, Robert. Either get her out of this house, or your child and I will leave," Gwen snapped. She was getting fed up with Leah's presence more than before. The closer her pregnancy due date came, the more she wanted the woman out of their lives.

Robert went pale, shocked by her ultimatum. "You wouldn't do such a thing!"

"Watch me, Robert. Just watch me. Make your decision. The clock is ticking."

Seeing he was ready to argue some more, she stormed out of the room, almost running into Leah. She glared at her, pretty sure she'd been listening in. Gwen, however, didn't care. It was good that Leah knew there was an ultimatum. She hadn't wanted to force him to choose, but she'd been pushed too far. Robert would pick her and their child. He knew she wasn't bluffing; he knew what she was capable of. As much as he cared for his ex-wife, he cared more for Leah and their unborn child more. She patted her stomach in pleasure, and her baby moved in response. She felt she and her child were going to make a perfect team.

A few days later, she met Danielle, Gabby, and Trina at a nearby restaurant. Gwen had gained a lot of weight, so she didn't go out much, limiting her outings.

"It took every bit of my energy to get ready today, and I can't wait to have this baby," Gwen admitted as she joined the table. She was the last to arrive because her dumb driver had taken a wrong turn.

"You look radiant," Gabby said.

This made her beam. Then her eyes settled on a woman. Who was she? She blinked. No way! "Danielle, is that you?"

Danielle laughed at the surprised look she wore. "Come on; you girls act like I don't look the same."

"You don't," Trina said.

The hair-color change made her look different, younger. Now she looked more her age than like a stuffy old lady. She was even showing a bit of cleavage. Well, well, it had taken a cheating husband to make Danielle revamp.

"You notified us of some changes in your style, but I didn't expect this," Gwen said. "What did Brad say?"

"He was surprised. He kept staring at me for a few minutes, and then he seemed angry." Danielle frowned as she ran her fingers through her hair. "I don't know why he's upset.

The women he slept with had all sorts of hair colors. One would think he would want his wife to be like them."

"The Madonna-whore syndrome," Trina said before taking a long sip from her glass.

"What's that?" Danielle asked.

"Something about a man wanting a whore and an angel at the same time?" Gwen said.

"Kind of. It translates to men wanting the best of both worlds. They want a wife who can cook and maintain the household and a mistress who does any fetish they want," Trina continued.

"Well, whatever syndrome he wants, I told him I'm not changing my hair back to how it was. I like it this way," Danielle said, tossing her hair to the other side of her head.

"Have you decided what to do with him?" Gabby asked. She had returned a few weeks ago from a trip to the Maldives. Dave had taken some time off work, and they had gone for some alone time after the debacle that happened with Dave's former girlfriend Diana, who slept with his father, had a child, and tried to pin the child on him.

"I spoke to my cousin Julia and had her review the merger agreement. Let's say there's a clause that gives me an out, but I don't know what to do or how to run the company. I don't even know if I want it," Danielle lamented.

Gwen rolled her eyes. Danielle might as well keep her husband in charge until he runs the company to the ground, catering to his mistresses and paying all their expenses.

"I don't think running a company will be that difficult. Right, Trina?" Gabby asked.

"Well, it is difficult. Running my business can be overwhelming, but you'll figure it out. Millions of women are running businesses worldwide, and they're not dropping dead on the streets," Trina said to Danielle.

"If Crazy can do it, so can you," Gwen added. She earned a glare from Danielle and a chuckle from the others. The "Crazy" she was referring to was Lori, now the executive head of her company, against all odds, mainly consisting of opposition from the board of directors. No one knew what had happened to Greg except the parties involved, which included Trina, Gwen, Danielle, Gabby, and, of course, Lori. And while there were whispers that Lori had gotten rid of him, there was no proof. The cops had gone to the house, searched the premises, and found nothing incriminating. The question on many minds was, where was Greg? Many suspected he was dead, but his disappearance remained a mystery. Lori seemed not to care about it and continued with her life.

"How are things with Charles?" Gabby asked.

Trina sighed at this, making Gwen roll her eyes. She wondered what was so tricky about calling things off with the man. Either she did that or married him, regardless of not loving him or his awful mother. He had money. That was what should matter. She was pretty sure Trina could manipulate him to do whatever she wanted.

"He called me this morning. He wants us to take a trip to some resort next weekend. You know what that means? He wants to propose," Trina said.

"Are you going with him?" Danielle asked.

"And have to turn down his proposal? Hell no! I haven't

done that to anyone, and I'm not about to do so. I'm going to end things with him before next weekend." Trina took a long sip from her glass.

"I don't know, but I feel trouble is brewing for one of us, and it will explode in our faces," Gabby said, looking around with a worried expression.

"Is this about the dream you had?" Trina asked.

"I've had it three times now. My grandma used to say something about recurring dreams, that they are bound to happen," Gabby said. Gwen scoffed. Next, Gabby would want to see a priest to interpret her dreams. "Do you know how often I have dreamed of kicking Leah out of my house?"

"I feel we should be careful. I can never remember the details of the dreams, but I know one of us is in trouble. Someone wanted to hurt us. We need to be careful in whatever we do," Gabby advised.

"Yeah, right," Gwen muttered to herself.

GABBY

Dave was home when Gabby returned. Her heart leaped in excitement as she walked into their bedroom and saw him. Ever since the incident with Diana, they had bonded more than before. He had been the one to suggest they go on a trip, and for over a month, he had spent most of his free time with Gabby, exploring the islands and making plans for the future.

On their return, nothing had changed; they were still as close as before. What had seemed like it would destroy her marriage had succeeded in bringing them closer.

"My mother called," Dave said with a grimace. He still wasn't speaking with his parents, and Gabby supported him. What his parents had done, especially his father, had been horrible. To sleep with your son's girlfriend was just crazy! Dave had felt guilt about hurting Diana for years, and now that burden was off his shoulders. However, Dave cared for the child that had emerged from the union, and although Dave had tried to reach out to Diana, she had turned down his efforts to provide for his brother. Hopefully, when his brother, Adrian, grew up and became an adult, he would reach out to Dave. Otherwise, there wasn't anything he could do.

"When will you talk to your parents?" Gabby asked.

Dave shrugged. "When I'm up to it. In a way, I have forgiven them, but I'm still pissed with my father for what he did. I don't know when I'll be able to talk to them without getting upset."

She rested her head on his chest, and he wrapped his arms around her. "How are your friends?" he asked.

Pulling away, she said, "Well, Gwen is Gwen. Ready to pop any day, and I fear for the after-birth Gwen. Pregnancy made her more relaxed, and she might worsen after giving birth. Danielle is… doing great. She dyed her hair blonde, and she looked hot. And Trina must break a man's heart before next weekend."

Dave chuckled at this. "That sucks!"

Gabby had met Charles a few times, and he seemed like a great guy; however, she didn't think he was great for Trina. He cared for her, no doubt, but he was too passive, and Trina would get tired of him. She needed someone who was strong like she was. Someone who wasn't still controlled by his mother. And that someone wasn't Charles.

Gabby reflected on the recurring dreams she had started having when they returned home. It irked her that she couldn't recall the details. Her friends dismissed her, and while she wasn't spiritual, she could feel it in her bones that something terrible would happen to one of them. She only wondered why she didn't have these dreams months ago before all the stuff with Dave and his family occurred. Interesting.

"What's wrong? You have that worried look on your face," Dave said.

"No one takes the dreams I'm having seriously," Gabby said with a pointed look as Dave looked away. He, too, thought she was overreacting.

"I'm guessing your friends paid no mind to it."

"Exactly! I'm worried about everyone here, and you all think I'm crazy." Gabby glared.

He placed his hands on her shoulders. "No one thinks you're crazy but having a recurring nightmare doesn't mean something terrible will happen to you or your friends. It's just a dream and nothing more."

Gabby sighed. Usually, she wasn't so bothered about things like this, but something about this dream unnerved her. But she guessed the others were right; there wasn't anything

to worry about. However, she was going to be careful.
And she hoped the others would be as well.

CHAPTER THREE

TRINA & GWEN

"You're going to break up with me, aren't you?" Charles asked.

Trina nodded. There was no need to deny it. He could see it coming. In the past week, she had pulled away from him, not returning his calls, ignoring him, all in the process of completely ghosting him. They were supposed to be heading to the resort in a few days, but she had told him she was too busy and couldn't make it.

"I thought as much," Charles said with a deep sigh. "You've been giving me the cold shoulder over the past few weeks, trying to end things with me gradually. Why? Is it because of my mom? I know she doesn't like you. I also know she got you kicked out of your old building." He saw the surprise on her face and said, "Yes, I know; I stumbled across the papers to the building. I know she doesn't want you around me, but that doesn't mean you should listen to her. I'm my own man!"

"This isn't about your mother. This is about us." It was usually easy to end relationships with men. But she had developed feelings for him. That wasn't enough to make her stay, but it was enough for her not to hurt him.

"I love you, Trina; I've told you this several times."

"And I have a soft spot for you." Almost immediately, she wished she could take back her words. The hurt was clear in his eyes.

"You're strong to a fault, Trina! You don't give others the opportunity of loving you as they should. Whenever you think someone is getting too close, you push them away." Charles reached for her, pulling her to him. "Please, think about us. Don't get rid of what we have. We're good together. You know this."

She pulled away from him. This wasn't going to be easy. This was the worse breakup she had ever initiated. "What you want is a wife and children. And, yes, I know you'll propose to me over the weekend."

He looked surprised, for an instance. "My mother!" he spat. "I'm not ready for that."

"But you'll make a great wife and mother."

Maybe she would, and maybe she wouldn't. "Like I said, I'm not ready for that. Look, Charles, you're a great guy and all, and we had fun, but I'm not going to be your wife. Go marry some girl who fits into your circle, like Michelle."

Charles took a deep breath and sat on the couch, his head buried in his hands. Just as she wondered if she would have to tell him to leave, he stood up.

"Contrary to what you think, we are good together. Think about this for a few days before ending us." He placed a finger on her lips before she could tell him she had made her decision. "Please, Trina, rethink this. And know that I love you." He kissed her before heading out the door.

She felt horrible as the door closed behind him; she felt like crying. Damn! Trina should have kicked him out before things became too intense between them. However, it wasn't too late for her to nurse her heart.

She was going to miss him, no doubt. He had been a great boyfriend and lover, but now it was time to move on. She was going to take a vacation from men. No men. Not even a one-night stand. It would just be her and her business for the next couple of months. Any itch she felt, she was going to handle it by herself.

She had set Charles free, but that didn't mean his mother had won because the mommy's boy Trina had started dating was different from the man she had just ended things with. They both had grown in their relationship, and she took joy in knowing she had helped break the chains holding him back. Hopefully, the next woman he dated would enjoy her hard work and be free from his mother's manipulation. In the meantime, she was going to heal. Perhaps she would go on a vacation. But then she would be distracted, she warned herself. Vacation meant there would be tempting men, which might break her resolve.

"Should never have dated him!" They should have remained friends. But she couldn't go back and change the past.

It was over with Charles, even if he thought she would change her mind. She wouldn't. That chapter of her life was sadly over.

She headed to the kitchen and grabbed her favorite whiskey, which she consumed from the bottle. She choked at the hot taste as it hit her throat.

Her phone buzzed. It was her girlfriend Keisha, who owned a beauty salon.

"Hey, friend, you want to party this weekend?" Keisha asked in an excited voice. "The Cat Meow club is hosting its grand opening. It's going to be lit!"

Partying meant men dancing around Trina, and she didn't want that.

"Not this weekend. I'm busy," Trina said. "Damn, girl! Your loss!"

She was indeed getting soft. The old Trina wouldn't give a shit, and hours after a breakup, she would have been partying wild. Damn Charles!

GWEN

Gwen knew it! She had known Leah was up to no good, and the evidence proved it. After weeks of intense surveillance, the PI had discovered the truth. The only thing Leah was suffering from was evil. It coursed through her blood veins.

The documents he had sent to Gwen were top secret; they weren't supposed to exist, but the doctor left a paper trail, perhaps for his own protection or benefit.

Her eyes raked through them again. The doctor had detailed everything that had happened in the confidential report. A few months ago, Leah had contacted him through an unmentioned third party and made an appointment with him, where she requested that he forge results for her and aid her with undergoing fake cancer treatments. They had negotiated a fee, and he had set the plan into motion. He had provided her with the necessary medication and detailed information on the signs and symptoms exhibited by cancer patients. Every time she went for treatments, she was really working out extensively.

It was incredible the lengths Leah would go to remain in their lives! Now she was in big trouble, and so was that crappy doctor. Gwen had always wondered why Leah didn't go to her usual doctors but to some small clinic instead. Now the answer was clear.

She was such a freaking bitch! Acting like she was ill. She was even shaving off her hair. Come on! Gwen had known she was a scheming old witch! She deserved an Oscar for her near-perfect performance, but Gwen had known better.

She perked up at the noise of a car pulling up in front of the house. It was Robert returning from one of the so-called treatments with Leah. Stupid Robert, he had fallen for her act. He had always been naïve. But at least this would open his eyes. She wouldn't let a moment pass before she exposed the truth; he needed to know how horrible his ex-wife was. The thousands of dollars Gwen had spent were indeed worth it.

She thought briefly about what Blake, Robert's nephew,

had said about Leah being calculative and worse than Gwen could comprehend. He had been damn right. The woman was crazy! She needed to be locked in a mental facility.

Her heels smacking against the marble tiles, she descended the stairs, wearing a broad smile.

"Gwen," Robert said as she walked into view. Leah held on to him, wearing a tired look.

"How was the treatment today?" Gwen asked.

"Tense. Today wasn't a good day for Leah; she needs to get some rest," Robert said.

"Please take me to my room, Robert," Leah whispered.

Gwen rolled her eyes. Damn, she was a freaking good actress! The woman barely broke character.

With the file in her hand, she had no choice but to give a resounding applause. Robert and Leah looked at her, confused, and then Leah's eyes narrowed.

"You're an amazing actress. When Robert kicks you out of this house, you know, you should go to Hollywood. With your botoxed face, you might make it there," Gwen sneered.

"Gwen!" Robert snapped. "I just told you Leah has had a bad day.

I have had it with you!"

"Ignore her," Leah pleaded and continued with a low voice. "Please take me to my room."

"Not so fast!" Gwen said as they walked past her. "Robert, I have something interesting to show you now."

"That can wait; I need to get Leah settled in bed."

"Are you sure you want to wait? Because this concerns Leah." Gwen giggled as the woman glared at her, now slightly concerned. "You see, I wasn't convinced of Leah's little act of being sick, so I hired a private investigator." Anger flashed in Robert's eyes, and she quickly moved on. "And he had a lot to reveal. A lot that will interest you." She waved the file in the air.

"Robert, let's go! Please, I'm weak," Leah winced.

"If you like, you can pass out, but today's truth will be revealed." Gwen smiled, reading through her theatrics.

"Robert, please don't believe anything she says. I don't know what she's talking about," Leah rasped.

Gwen extended the file toward him.

"I…." He pulled away from Leah, and Gwen happily gave him the file.

"Robert, I'm feeling dizzy." Leah pressed her hand to her head as Robert flipped the file open. However, he ignored her; his eyes stuck to the words on the first page.

"Robert, please…."

"Shut up, Leah!" Robert snapped.

Silence descended, and Gwen swore she could hear Leah's heart beating as she glared at her in a fury. Gwen half expected her to attack, trying to claw her while he read the file.

Robert took a deep breath and closed his eyes. When he opened them, there was so much hurt in them that Gwen almost wished she hadn't told him the truth. It was going to break him. She quickly consoled herself. Leah was supposedly his good friend of over thirty years. Her husband shouldn't be close friends with a woman other than her. It was time for Leah to be gone from their lives.

"Is this true, Leah?" Robert asked in the coldest voice

Gwen had ever heard. It sent chills down to her toes.

"Robert, I don't know what's in there, but I can explain. They're all lies. Don't believe Gwen. You know she wants me out of this house," Leah pleaded.

"So, if I call the authorities right now, and they go over to the clinic, they won't discover that you have been faking having cancer?" Robert asked.

Leah went quiet. Then she said, "I'm sorry, Robert! I'm so sorry!" She burst into tears and reached for him, but he pulled away.

"You're sorry for lying to me? For pretending that you have cancer? For having me worried that you were going to die? You're sorry about all of that?" Robert asked quietly.

"Please, Robert. I didn't want to do it, but she made me do it!" She glared at Gwen.

"Me? I told you to pretend that you had cancer?" Gwen folded her arms over her chest.

"You pushed me to it!" Leah snapped. "You have attacked me from the first day!"

She had done so because she knew she was an annoying person! Who got to be friends with the ex-wife? That only happened on *Dynasty*, not in real life.

"You have always competed with me!" Leah continued.

Gwen shook her head while disagreeing with her. There was no competition. Leah couldn't stand on the same footing as Gwen.

"You made me do this! You're the cause of this!" Leah yelled.

Calmly, Gwen said, "Don't blame me, Leah. You're solely

responsible for all of this. You walked into this knowingly. You're crazy and need help."

"I'm not crazy!" Leah's eyes flashed.

Gwen had meant it as a jab, but now she suspected the woman was crazy. Only a mentally deranged person would even think of such a plan to start with.

"I want you to go upstairs and get all your belongings, Leah.

Everything," Robert instructed.

Tears welled in Leah's eyes, and Gwen scoffed. *Yeah, right.*

"Get your things and leave my house, Leah, before I do something I will regret." With that, Robert walked off.

The tears quickly vanished as Leah turned to her. Gwen felt a sudden sense of dread as the woman's eyes locked on her. She took a step backward, and Leah moved toward her. Leah grabbed her by the arm before she could comprehend what was happening.

"Let go of me, you crazy bitch!" Gwen struggled.

"You haven't won, bimbo. You have no idea the plans I have for you. You destroyed my marriage, and I will make you pay." Her laughter sent chills through Gwen's body, and she pulled away.

Warily, she watched Leah walk away. The woman's words echoed in her thoughts. That had been a serious threat. What was Leah up to? She hadn't looked as bothered as she should have been. Only someone with a more sinister plan wouldn't be disturbed.

Gwen found Robert in the study drinking from a bottle of rum he usually turned to when a business deal failed. She stood in the doorway watching him. He was hurting from Leah's betrayal. As much as she didn't want to be responsible for breaking the news to him, he needed to know the truth. There was no way she could have continued with Leah playing her husband like a fiddle. Not on her watch.

He would eventually heal, and she would be there for him. As well as their child. The baby stirred in agreement. In a few weeks, she would pop the brat out, and Robert would be distracted. That nasty Leah would soon be a memory of the past.

A few hours later, she watched from her bedroom window as Leah drove away, her bags in her car. Gwen hoped she hadn't left anything behind because she wasn't welcome back. She wished she could toast to Leah's departure.

Finally! After years of putting up with her, Leah had dug her grave and was no longer in their lives. However, as she pulled away from the window, her sense of victory faltered at the memory of Leah's departing words. Gabby's dreams resurfaced for a moment, but she quickly squashed them. Leah was gone from their lives for good.

CHAPTER FOUR

DANIELLE

Danielle's courage dwindled for a moment at the sight of Brad. Despite her friends' encouragement over the past few days and her lawyer's presence, she was worried about the outcome of today. Could she really go through with this?

Today was the general meeting of stakeholders at the company. It was the day she would announce playing an active role in the company.

"What are you doing here?" Brad asked in surprise as she walked into his office with Julia.

"I can't attend a meeting in my company?" Danielle replied. "You have never attended any meeting."

"Things have changed. I will be playing an active role in the company from henceforth," Danielle informed her husband.

Brad frowned. "What do you mean?"

"That I will be playing an active role in the company?" Danielle asked.

"Did you put her up to this, Julia?" Brad questioned.

"No, I made the decision on my own," Danielle explained.

"Why don't you go home, and when I return, we'll talk? You won't understand anything said in the meeting," Brad pushed.

"I'm going to attend the meeting, Brad. I'll see you there."

She could sense Brad's disapproval as they left the office. He didn't want them around, but there wasn't anything he could do about it. They were going to attend the meeting whether he liked it or not.

The meeting was an eye-opener. All of the stakeholders were surprised to see her, so the first few minutes were spent with everyone looking her way in confusion. She had to prompt Brad to introduce her. When the meeting finally started and the reports were discussed, she was shocked to discover that, while the company wasn't failing, it wasn't doing great either. They had experienced significant losses, and changes were necessary. She attempted to voice her opinion, but Brad and his father found a way to ignore her every time she did. It was so embarrassing that she stopped making suggestions. Danielle was fuming on the inside. They had tried to make her seem incompetent by ignoring her and talking over her. How dare they deliberately undermine her? She could feel the anger radiating off Julia, but she signaled to her not to interfere. They would sort it out afterward.

"When my parents' company merged with your father's, the agreement was for my parents to take control. But since they decided to retire, they wanted to put me in charge. At that time, I had no wish to do so, so I allowed you to be the CEO, and I didn't mind you bringing your dad on board to provide oversight. But the way you both treated me in the meeting, I didn't like it," Danielle told her husband when they returned to his office.

"How did I treat you?" Brad asked innocently. "You undermined me. Made a fool of me."

"Does she have to be here?" Brad nodded at Julia, who was watching them.

"Yes. She's my lawyer."

His brow lifted. "Your lawyer? What do you need a lawyer for?" "To get control of the company," Danielle said with a shrug.

His mouth dropped open; then, he burst into laughter. "Are you… are you joking?"

"No, I'm not. Julia is my lawyer, and it is my company as I am the majority stockholder, right, Julia?" Danielle asked.

"Right."

Brad's eyes narrowed. "Is there something you're not telling me? Why would you want that? I run this company well. We had an agreement that you would stay at home while I take over your family company."

"First, we never had an agreement. It was just an assumption. I wasn't interested in running the company then, but now I am. Is there anything wrong with that?"

They were interrupted by a knock on the door before Danielle's father-in-law, Mitch, walked in. "What are you doing here, Danielle?" he asked, not wasting time.

"Why don't you fill your father in?" Danielle asked, rubbing the sides of her head. She could feel a headache kicking in. "Julia and I will go walk around the company."

While the ladies were walking around, Danielle's phone rang. It was Brad. He and his father wanted to talk to her. Alone. However, she returned with Julia behind her.

"Excuse us, Julia," Mitch commanded.

Danielle nodded at Julia to step outside. She would be able to deal with this without caving.

"What's this stunt you're pulling?" Mitch snapped. "Do you know how embarrassing this is? To have you here?"

"What's embarrassing is you trying to shut me down every time I suggested a solution. I won't accept that next time," Danielle said sternly.

"What is this, Danielle? Why are you here?" Mitch demanded.

Danielle folded her arms. Her presence seemed to be upsetting them. Her eyes narrowed on them. They didn't want her around.

"Brad must have filled you in, right?" Danielle asked.

"Your place is in the house, Danielle. What do you know about business, huh? It would help if you concerned yourself with how to give your husband children," Mitch berated.

Danielle winced at his harsh, misogynistic words. The man had no filter and didn't care about other people's feelings. However, she had tough skin—or, rather, she was developing one.

"I'm not going back and forth with you, Mitch. There's no negotiation with this. I—"

"Who's feeding your head with nonsense? Is it Lori? Do you think because she wears some stupid pantsuit every day, that makes her the boss?" Mitch ranted.

Danielle had had it with the old geezer. "Shut your fucking mouth, Mitch. Shut it!"

Both her husband and father-in-law went pale. Danielle never got angry, but she couldn't take it any longer.

"I'm not backing down from this. I have watched you run this company the way you want, but not any longer. I have a say in what this company does, and no one's changing that. If you don't like it, get the hell out of here." She turned and stormed out, slamming the door behind her.

She felt a surge of energy as she joined Julia. She had made it clear to them that she wasn't a pushover.

She saw calls from her parents when she got home, but she refused to return them. Brad and his father must have called them to tell on her like she was five or something. She regretted not standing up to them, her family, and Brad sooner. However, it was better late than never. She loved her newfound confidence, and she wasn't backing down.

That evening, she anticipated Brad's return. He had been busy at "work" lately, barely spending time at home in the last few months. And, of course, she had let him be. There was no need to worry about him when she knew he was in the arms of another woman.

"I want you to tell me what's happening with you," Brad said, handing her a bunch of red flowers. They smelled nice, but she discarded them for what they were—a bribe.

"What do you mean?"

"Your coming to the company with a lawyer. Don't you trust me?"

"Why do you think I don't trust you?" she threw back at him. "Well… I've noticed you pulling away from me."

She laughed at this. He'd noticed her pulling away. How touching!

"Is there something you want to share with me?" Brad asked, seeming concerned.

"Brad, I've been in the shadows for years, letting everyone oppress me. I refuse to let that happen anymore."

"So, this is a midlife crisis? With the hair change. The clothes. Do you want to see a therapist? You could go away for a while."

"I know you've been cheating on me."

Brad went completely quiet as he shrugged off his tie and headed to the drink bar, returning with a glass of whiskey. "How long have you known?"

Danielle shrugged. "Does it matter?"

"I'm sorry, Danielle. It… it just happened. What Monica and I have is not serious. It's just a fling. Work was crazy one night, and… it just happened. It will never happen again. I'm going to end things with her right now."

He thought she was stupid, didn't he? And she had been, she had to admit. "Cut the act, Brad. I know you've been sleeping with different women. Monica isn't the first. You've messed around with Jessica and Cindy's friend too." She almost laughed as his face lost all color. His act was up.

"How… how…? You hired someone to follow me?"

Anger flashed in his eyes.

"Yes, I did. And I have a round figure of how many women you've been with since we married and how much you've spent on them, so don't put up an innocent act."

"How could you do such a thing?" Brad demanded.

"You're angry with me for finding out you've been cheating?" It was incredible that Brad would try to turn this around on her. How could she not have seen him for the selfish person he was?

"It is…." He took a deep breath. "I'm sorry, Danielle. I really am. But these things happen. You were not responsive in bed, and I had no option but to go to other women."

"And when I became responsive? Did the cheating stop?"
"I'm sorry, Danielle."

"You're not sorry, Brad. The only reason you're saying this is because I caught you cheating. You might be faithful for the next couple of months, but you'll return to your cheating ways."

He looked away, knowing she was right. "I love you," he blurted. Her heart winced in pain. He had never told her that, and although she knew he cared for her somehow, she couldn't let him

manipulate her emotionally.

"We can work this out. We'll go to couples therapy. We'll spend more time together. I promise you I won't cheat again."

"I need some space from you," Danielle heard herself saying and realized it was true. Despite him not being around much anyway, she needed to get away from him completely to give herself time to think things through. She'd been focused on him and others for most of her life, so she had forgotten about herself. It was time for her.

"You want a divorce?" Brad croaked. "I don't know. I need some time."

He looked wounded, and she wasn't sure if he was faking it. She wished she didn't love him; it would have been easier for her.

"I'll get my things and leave," Brad said. As he made to move past her, he stopped. "I know I've hurt you, Danielle. A lot. I broke your trust and love, but I'm sorry. I don't want to lose you. Don't give up on us, please."

Tears welled in her eyes as she heard him go up the stairs.

It was sad how their marriage had been reduced to this. They had never been crazy in love, but she had believed they had the utmost respect for each other. And while she had lived up to the expectations of marriage, he hadn't.

As he got into his car with a bag, she wondered if this was the end of their union.

CHAPTER FIVE

GWEN & TRINA

Gwen was a mother. She looked in disbelief at the baby next to her. It still seemed surreal. She had given birth to a healthy baby two weeks earlier than her supposed due date.

She had yelled at the annoying doctor all through the delivery process.

She winced as she recalled the birth of her child. She doubted she would want to repeat it. It had been so painful, and she still felt weak hours later. However, there was a sudden love that hadn't ceased for her daughter.

She was just so beautiful. And perfect, with all her fingers and limbs intact. Gwen had instructed the doctor several times to examine her thoroughly to ensure nothing was wrong with her before they took her home. However, contrary to her earlier stance, if something was wrong with her, she was still going home with her. She doubted she could ever leave her child.

It was crazy how strongly she felt for her child, Fiona. There was a bond she couldn't explain. And she was going to ensure she had the best life. Fiona was going to lack nothing.

"She's beautiful," Robert said.

He looked tired, as he should be. He had been up all day and by her side since the contractions started. He'd insisted on being with her in the delivery room, and she had worried he would pass out at one point.

Robert was going to be a great father. He'd been reading books on fatherhood and had even joined her in birthing classes. Seeing him hold their child had brought tears to her eyes. Getting pregnant was the best decision she had ever made.

He had been feeling down since Leah left, more down than she had anticipated. However, as her due date drew closer, she got him more involved. Now that their child was here, she was sure Leah would be a thing of the past for him. Because for Gwen, Leah was out of their lives. The woman had left town and moved to her country home, where she should have been in the first place. Robert hadn't told anyone of her deceit, and, well, to respect him, Gwen had kept her mouth closed, although she wanted to yell the truth to everyone. They should all know how despicable Leah was.

"Your friends are here to see you," Robert informed her.

"Wait! Don't let them in yet! How do I look?" She dashed to the mirror.

Robert chuckled. "You look beautiful as always."

He was right. Delivery had done nothing to alter Gwen's looks.

She still looked great, as always.

The door opened, and her friends walked in with gifts. A smile spread on her lips. She was so happy to see them. Friends were usually annoying and competitive, but she cared about this group. They had gone through crazy experiences, bringing them closer to each other.

"Oh my God! She's so gorgeous!" Gabby cried, looking into the cradle.

"She looks so much like her father." Trina beamed.

"Hey!" Gwen growled, glaring at her friend. No, Fiona looked like her.

Everyone laughed, and Gwen dissolved into a smile.

"You made a lovely baby, Gwen. You and Robert," Danielle said. "Thank you, ladies. I'll step outside for a few minutes and give you some time," Robert said, excusing himself. "So, how do you feel?" Trina asked.

"Like my body has been ripped into two from the inside," Gwen said. "In a few days, I have an appointment with a doctor, a masseuse, and a therapist. Whew! I need to heal from the outside to the inside." Danielle chuckled. "I can't believe you're really a mom. But you'll make a great mom—an annoying one, but a great and protective one."

The other women nodded in agreement. Now Gwen felt like crying. She appreciated their support more than she could admit. They were the closest people in her life, and she could share anything with them.

"How's work?" Gwen asked Danielle.

"Great. It's not as easy as I thought it would be. There's so much to learn, but it's a challenge I'm taking on." In the past month, Danielle went to the company almost every workday, learning the ropes. As she said, it was tough for her, but she wasn't backing down. "Well, I have good news. Fiona will soon have a playmate," Gabby said.

The room first went quiet, and then everyone excitedly spoke at once.

"No way!"

"You're pregnant!" "Damn, girl!"

Gabby laughed heartily. "I know, I know. I found out last week that I'm two months along. With the past miscarriages, I didn't want to share this, but Dave and I have been to the doctor, and hopefully, this pregnancy will be problem-free."

"That's amazing news. I hope it's a boy," Gwen said. "I want a girl," Gabby said.

"It will be a boy," Gwen said with a glare. "A girl," Gabby countered.

They couldn't keep it up any longer, and they burst into laughter.

Gwen felt so good in the company of amazing friends who would be there for her through thick and thin. She had the perfect life that many out there wished for. She had an amazing husband and a newborn child she couldn't wait to spoil.

A few days later, Gwen was home with the baby. She was glad to be out of the annoying hospital with its horrible food and be back home with help at her beck and call. Robert had hired a live-in nanny and a nurse, but Gwen would be raising her child. Contrary to what she had thought, she wasn't going to relegate the upbringing of her daughter to the help. Unless

Fiona turned out to be a pest or the newness of having a child wore off.

There were a lot of guests in the first week, and she tried to accommodate them even if she would rather be left alone.

"She's beautiful," Blake said. He had stopped by with a huge pink teddy bear for the child.

Gwen had taken Fiona to her room with Blake in tow with the bear. They hadn't spoken for a while, except for a call when Leah had been kicked out of the house. Thinking of Leah made her grimace. Thank goodness she wasn't around when Fiona was born. Gwen's mood would have been soiled.

"Leah?" Blake asked, reading her thoughts.

"Yeah. I'm so glad she's out of our lives, but you never told me what happened between the two of you that made you dislike her."

Blake shrugged. "There's no need to revisit the past. But I saw her for the manipulative person she is, despite coming off as fragile."

There he went again with his secrets. Hopefully, one day he would give her the dirt on Leah to hold as more ammunition.

"Have you heard anything about her?" she asked.

Gwen knew Robert had asked about her a couple of times, but their mutual friends refused to share any information, which was good. They also gave Gwen dirty looks, believing she had something to do with Robert cutting Leah off. But she didn't care. After all, they were all a bunch of lowlifes, and what they thought of her didn't matter.

T R I N A

Trina was in a good mood. She was hopeful that nothing was going to ruin her day. Her new orders had flown off the racks with several preorders coming in, meaning she had to restock sooner than expected.

"Hello, Trina."

She rolled her eyes at Andre's voice. He had been hitting on her for a while, and she paid him no mind. He was too cocky and irritated her with his macho attitude. Trina didn't want any part of that. Ever since Charles, she hadn't dated, though she'd had a couple of one- night stands, ending with her turning down any offers for breakfast. She had no interest in getting into the dating pool after that stint with Charles. Trina did miss him, though. Last she heard, he had left the country against his mother's pleas.

"Come on, Trina. Let's go on a date. The best restaurant in town," Andre pushed on.

Just as she was about to cuss him out, her phone rang. It was Gwen. She froze at the sobbing she heard when she answered the phone. Gwen was incoherent.

"Calm down, Gwen. Please, I need you to calm down. What are you saying?" Trina asked.

"Someone took Fiona. Someone kidnapped my daughter!"

"I'm on my way!"

Trina grabbed her car keys and was out of her office, her heart pounding fast. What the fuck was going on? This had to happen just as things were beginning to work themselves out. Who would take the child? Fuck! Gwen had to be damn devastated. Being a mother had softened her, giving her more patience. Trina's hands squeezed around the steering wheel. Whoever took the child was in big trouble.

There were several police cruisers present when Trina pulled up to the house. She wasn't allowed in and was about to call Gwen when the butler came around to talk to the cops. Spotting Trina, he immediately ushered her in. There were even more cops flooding the inside. She spotted Gabby and Danielle comforting a crying Gwen. Her heart winced in pain for her friend as she hurried over to her.

Gwen hugged her tight as she sobbed.

"I'm so sorry, Gwen, but we'll get Fiona back. I promise you," Trina assured her. She couldn't imagine carrying a child for nine months only for it to be kidnapped in the first month after being born.

"I want my baby back," Gwen cried.

"And you will get her back. What happened?" Trina asked.

Gabby was the one who explained what had happened. A few guests had come over, and Gwen had attended to them while Fiona slept in her room. When she went to bring the child down, she wasn't in her cot. She hadn't been with the nurse or nanny either. They had searched through the house, but Fiona hadn't been found.

"Leah," Trina said.

Gwen nodded, her eyes flashing with rage. "That fucking bitch took my daughter! She threatened me! I should have known she was crazy and wouldn't just let us be."

Gabby made the sign of the cross. Trina thought about the nightmares she'd had before Fiona was born, about something terrible happening to one of them. None of them had paid the dreams any attention, but now they had turned into a reality.

"Have the cops located Leah?" Trina asked.

"They're on the way to her house right now. If she lays a finger on my child, Trina, I swear I will kill her!" Gwen snarled with a such steeliness that Trina didn't doubt her words.

"We're going to kill her," Trina corrected. And she didn't mind going to jail for doing it. Someone who kidnapped a kid deserved to die, in her opinion.

Robert walked into the room, and Gwen rushed to him. "I swear I will kill Leah if she does this!" Robert growled.

Join the club, Trina thought. The woman couldn't just take her loss and move on. Trina hoped Fiona would emerge from this unscathed.

The wait was excruciating, watching cops come and go. Trina was impressed by Gwen's strength. She had stopped crying, and now there was a calmness to her, yet she could feel her worry.

It was seven that evening when the detective in charge of the investigation returned. Danielle and Gabby had gone home, but Trina was staying the night.

"Did you find her?" Gwen asked, getting up.

"We found Leah, but she's not with the child. She has an alibi that checked out," the detective said.

"You idiot!" Gwen yelled. "Of course, the bitch has an alibi! Do you think she's going to make it easy for you? I want my daughter, you asshole. Leah took my daughter!"

Now Gwen was hysterical. Robert tried to hold on to her, but she broke into tears. Trina reached for her, comforting her.

"I want my daughter. I just want her," Gwen kept saying.

It took some sedatives for Gwen to calm down and be placed in bed. Trina turned to Robert, who had aged since that afternoon. He looked tired as hell.

"What's the next move?" Trina asked.

"It's time to bring in the big guns," Robert said.

Trina left early in the morning to get a change of clothes, pack a bag, and leave instructions for her store. By the time she headed back to Gwen's, it was almost noon. The cruisers had dwindled, but there were more vehicles with tinted windows, which she was curious about.

She knew from being from the streets of Detroit what Robert had meant by "big guns" when the door was opened by a man in a black suit. He had called in the FBI. She gave her name, which was on a list, and was allowed in. Danielle walked toward her.

"They called in the feds?" Trina asked.

"The feds and some special unit that deals in high-profile cases. The cops called in the feds, and Robert called in the special unit. But I feel like they're about to clash. Too much testosterone and too many egos are involved. And they're all hot," Danielle said.

Following her friend's gaze, Trina agreed with her. They were mostly good-looking and tall, with a dangerous aura. She smiled dreamily but quickly pulled herself back to reality. Gwen's child was in danger, so now wasn't the time for messing around. This was serious business.

"Any progress made?" Trina asked.

"No, but they're not ruling Leah out as a suspect," Danielle said. Despite the cops searching Leah's place and finding nothing incriminating, Trina was 100 percent sure that she was the one who took the child. No one could say anything else.

Gwen was dressed like a widow, in a black dress with a black hat on her head. Trina rolled her eyes at this. Her friend was so dramatic.

"How're you doing?" Trina asked.

"How do you expect me to be?" Gwen snapped.

Well, that had been a stupid question, Trina had to admit.

"I'm sorry," Gwen apologized, to Trina's surprise. "I just…. This is difficult for me. I'm worried about my daughter. I don't know where she is. I don't know who took her. I don't even know if she's still alive."

"We'll find her alive."

The voice made the hairs on Trina's body rise, and her toes curled in delight. She turned around and lifted a brow. The man standing before her was fucking hot! He was all shades of chocolate ice cream, and she barely resisted a growl. Who the hell was he?

"You're Trina?" he asked, his gorgeous eyes settling on her. "I am."

"Come with me. There are questions I need to ask you."

The fantasies flew out the window with that commanding and annoying tone he used. *Come with me"? Who the hell is he?* She didn't care how hot he was; if he was going to talk to her like she was five, then he was the ugliest man out there.

He gave her a look when she refused to budge. "You didn't say please," Trina pointed out.

He gave her a look. "A child is missing. I don't have time to deal with frivolities. Now come with me, and let me ask you a couple of questions so I can do my job."

Trina turned to Gwen. "I love you, girl, but this man will not like what happens next if he doesn't shut his mouth."

The man looked at his watch. "When you're ready to talk, inform one of the men." With that, he bounced off with Trina shooting daggers at him. He was so damn disrespectful! Who did he think he was?

"It's not just you, Trina. He was plain rude to me, like he suspected me or something. You should hear the questions he threw at me," Danielle said.

"Who the hell is he?" Trina snapped at Gwen.

"His name is Darrell. He's a former SEAL and owns a million- dollar tech company. He went to Robert's alma mater, and he came highly recommended. He always delivers. Always. Don't mess this up. Be kind to him," Gwen added with a pointed look.

Trina scoffed. *Yeah, right. Not to that annoying asshole!* He could take his handsomeness and shove it up his ass.

CHAPTER SIX

GWEN, DANIELLE, TRINA, & GABBY

Gwen could not describe how she was feeling. She was tired. She was worried. She was devastated. It was a surprise that she wasn't sedated in bed all day with all that was happening. Well, she knew why. She couldn't portray weakness. She couldn't let her enemies see her down. Never!

It still seemed like a dream that her daughter had been taken from the house. Never would she have imagined something like this would happen. Their home was safe, and they had only bothered with security cameras on the outside. However, the person who had taken Fiona had erased them. The cops were working hard to get information from them.

This was day four of her child's disappearance, and she was getting more worried, her bubble of strength crumbling. She thought of her daughter in the arms of a stranger. Or worse, dead. The latter she refused even to consider. The cops believed she was alive, but for how much longer? Getting her daughter back proved more difficult with every day that went by.

She was breaking on the inside, and so was Robert. He had become a shadow of himself. Their joy at becoming parents seemed to have been short-lived.

Leah! That conniving bitch! No matter what anyone told her, she knew Leah had something to do with this. The woman had gone for her daughter, knowing it would destroy her. If anything happened to Fiona, she was going to kill Leah. She didn't care. She would plead insanity.

The phones were tapped and monitored 24/7, but no ransom call was made. Worst of all, the kidnapping had been done so neatly that the cops could not find who Leah had sent to do the job. Even the so-called miracle workers Robert hired had found no clue. Perhaps they were just incompetent, which she believed.

Robert walked into the room with a grimace, and she jerked out of bed.

"What is it?" she asked.

"Leah is here. I tried to send her away, but she insists on being here."

"I don't want that bitch here! She took my child, and you know it!"

Robert nodded. "I know, Gwen. But right now, we don't know where she is. We need to be polite to her before she does something stupid." He took her hands, and she saw how tired he was. "I'm so sorry, Gwen, for not believing you. For letting her into our lives. I trusted her too much, and now she has decided to hurt us. If Leah took our child, I promise you I will make her pay."

The fury in his eyes was one she hadn't seen in years. It was one he reserved for his enemies, and she felt a bit of comfort with this. Robert would protect his family no matter what.

Leah was dressed in all black like the bitch was mourning. She wore her custom fragile expression, but Gwen saw right through it.

Trina, seated in the living room, shot her a look, and Gwen stifled a laugh; her friend was ready to start throwing punches once she gave the go-ahead.

"Oh, Gwen!"

Gwen moved away as Leah hurried to her side. "Don't touch me, Leah!" Gwen snapped.

For an instance, anger flashed in the woman's eyes. "I heard about your child. It's so sad what happened. For someone to come in here and take the baby, it's terrible! I don't know why the cops came to my house. I would never do such a thing to you. Why would I hurt you in such a way?" Leah asked innocently. For many reasons, Gwen had the family Leah had always wanted—Robert and a daughter.

Was she supposed to feel remorse for how she had treated Leah? Gwen didn't feel an ounce. All she felt was rage. But she forced herself to calm down. Her daughter's life was at stake, and she couldn't offend Leah. The woman was crazy and could do anything.

Darrell walked into the room, wearing the same frown as always.

He glanced at Leah for an instant and then at them.

"Gwen, I need to talk to you for a moment," Darrell said.

"I guess I should be going. I just came to give you my best wishes.

I'm sure you will be reunited as a family soon," Leah said.

Gwen wanted to wipe that smug look off Leah's face. She could hear the laughter in her voice. She wanted to deal with her badly, but that would wait until Fiona was home safely.

"Do you need me to follow the bitch and run her over?" Trina asked, joining them. This earned a glare from Darrell. The two had been at odds since they met, but Gwen didn't care. All that mattered now was her daughter.

"Excuse us," Darrell said.

Trina folded her arms. "I'm staying. Right, Gwen?"

"Let her stay. I trust her," Gwen said. It was true. She trusted her three friends more than she did most people in this room. They had been a huge support to her in the past few days.

"You shouldn't. Anyone could have kidnapped your daughter.

Anyone." Darrell pinned Trina with a look.

"I'm going to ignore that flimsy accusation you just threw at me," Trina snapped.

"What did you want to share with us?" Robert asked.

"We've gone through Leah's phone records, text messages, and finances going several months back. Nothing stands out as odd. No suspicious calls, movements, or purchases. Her alibi also checks out. As much as we want her to be guilty, we need to consider other suspects," Darrell said.

"No! Leah took my daughter!" Gwen said.

"Gwen is right. I know trouble, and that woman is guilty as hell!" Trina added.

"Of course," Darrell muttered. "Robert, Gwen, I understand that you have issues with Leah, but for the sake of your child, we must focus more resources on other suspects. It's possible someone took advantage of the hostility between you and Leah. A few months ago, Greg Hudson went missing, and no physical or electronic traces have been found to this day. You did business with him, right? Is there a way the cases might be connected?" Perhaps noticing the change in her attitude at the mention of Greg's name, Darrell turned toward her. "Gwen?"

Greg was history and had nothing to do with their lives. Or did he? Was Darrell right, and were they looking at the wrong suspect? She exchanged a look with Trina.

"Is there something you're not sharing?" Darrell asked.

"We were social with the Hudsons but nothing more," Gwen said.

"You're in the same tea party as his wife, Lori, right?" Amy, Darrell's partner, pointed out.

Gwen rolled her eyes. "I only hang out with them because I'm bored. Nothing connects Greg's disappearance with my baby," she defended.

"And why are you so sure?" Darrell asked, putting her on the spot. "You're giving me a headache! I need to lie down!" Gwen said, touching her head. Robert quickly pulled her into his embrace. "Stay with the cops and special units; I'll take her to her room,"

Trina said to Robert.

Gwen could feel Darrell's suspicious gaze as they escaped

to the bedroom. As soon as her door closed behind them, she turned to Trina.

"Do you think he's right? That this might have something to do with Greg? What if someone knows what we did and took Fiona to make us tell the truth?" Gwen asked.

"First, it doesn't make sense. They could have gone for any of us instead of waiting for you to give birth. Besides, I still have all my bets placed on Leah," Trina said.

"I don't know…. I really don't know. Darrell might be right. This might be a distraction to get us off the real kidnappers. Oh, God! I really don't care who took her. I just want my daughter back!"

"I promise you we will get her. Alive." Trina headed for the door. "Where are you going?"

Trina turned around. "We can't leave your daughter's fate to the cops. We'll find her on our own. You just wait here. Danielle, Gabby, and I will keep in touch."

As the door closed behind Trina, Gwen felt a sudden calm. Her friends would be looking for her daughter, and she trusted them more than the police.

DANIELLE

"So, I might be getting back with Brad," Danielle said. She received silence in response. "Aren't you guys going to say anything?" she asked, throwing a look at Trina, who was next to her in the passenger's seat.

"I expected it." Trina shrugged.

Gabby, who was eating a hamburger they had bought at a drive- through, mumbled with a mouthful, "Same."

"Seriously?"

Trina nodded. "You've been miserable without him. You dove into work, but a part of you feels like something's missing."

Trina was right. Danielle did miss Brad, especially when she saw him at the office almost every day. As much as she had tried to occupy herself with work, she felt lonely and sad.

The work was a challenge, a departure from the simple life she had lived prior, but she actually enjoyed it now. She had come to love the stress that came with it. But at night, she lay in bed thinking of Brad. She hated how much she loved him even after what he had done to her.

However, the feeling was mutual. He was miserable as well. He looked untidy and had this annoying beard she wanted him to get rid of.

Danielle and Brad had exchanged a few words in the past several months, although he did most of the talking. But yesterday, he had burst into her office and broken down, telling her he was sorry and wanted her back. He missed her, just as she missed him. Despite this, she had been stern with him, refusing to let him know she was a mess on the inside. They had agreed he would move back in, and they worked on their marriage while he continued with the therapy he had started going to. She hoped he wouldn't betray her again; she didn't know what she would do if he did. However, she was hopeful. It had taken her leaving to make him realize how much he cared for her. Perhaps they could work this out for real.

The car pulled into an empty slot in the parking lot of Solutions, the company once run by Greg but now by Lori. Danielle had called ahead of time, and Lori was expecting them. It still felt awkward to be around Lori, even though it seemed the woman had moved on. Now, she radiated confidence.

"I heard about Gwen's daughter. How's she doing?" Lori asked as they settled into chairs.

"Not great. She's on the brink of a breakdown. That's why we're here. Did you tell anyone about what happened?" Trina asked.

Lori frowned. "What happened?"

Gabby coughed, looking away. "You know, umm… what happened…."

"I don't know what you're talking about." Lori shook her head.

Gabby made a slicing gesture to her neck, and Lori laughed. "Just kidding. Of course, I can't forget, and I appreciate you ladies keeping quiet about it. I never told anyone. That's a secret I will take to the grave. Why?"

"Some douchebag cop thinks there's a link between the child's disappearance and Greg's," Trina said.

Lori's eyebrows furrowed. "I thought Leah took the child." "Exactly! But she has a clear alibi, and the cops are looking for alternate suspects," Danielle explained.

Lori scoffed. "Anyone can have a foolproof alibi; you must make the right plans ahead of time. I'm pretty sure Leah is responsible. That woman gives me the creeps. I've never been a fan of her."

Trina threw Danielle a look that made Danielle stifle a laugh. "And there's no way anyone would have found out the truth? Any traces?"

Lori smiled coldly. "I got rid of everything."

This statement sent a chill down Danielle's spine.

"People who commit crimes, like me," Lori added with a broad smile, "cover their tracks well. Think like a criminal, and you will catch one. But there are usually cracks, and you need to look out for them. Dig into Leah's past, and you'll find some clues." She looked at her wristwatch. "So, I guess I should be expecting the cops. Thanks for the tip-off."

Just as they walked into the foyer, Trina groaned. Danielle looked up and spotted Darrell and his partner headed their way.

"I thought you ladies weren't close to Lori," Darrell said sternly. "Umm…," Danielle began. She had to agree with Trina; the man was annoying.

"How again did you join the tea party?" Darrell examined her from head to toe.

Trina scowled. "Look, we don't have time for this line of questioning!" His partner gasped, and Trina glared at her. "I'll be in the car, ladies." And with that, she stormed off.

Danielle shot them an apologetic smile and hurried after Trina, glad to be out of Darrell's line of fire. The man's eyes were terrifying; it was like he could see right through her to the truth.

"That man is trouble," Gabby said as she caught up with them. "Big-time trouble, but we shouldn't concern ourselves with him. I really hope we're not wrong," Trina said. Talking to Lori had reconfirmed in their minds that Leah was responsible for the kidnapping.

Danielle hoped the same as well. Her friend's baby was out there, and she became more concerned for the child's fate with every second that went by.

CHAPTER SEVEN

GABBY

Gabby had not imagined her nightmares would manifest in such a way. She found herself constantly touching her stomach. She didn't know how she would react if her child were kidnapped. Gwen was indeed a strong woman.

A week had passed since Fiona went missing, and there were still no traces of the child. It was all over the news with a hefty reward amount offered. The calls came in from people who had no idea where the child was but were attracted to the reward money.

Gwen had just woken up from a long sleep when Gabby got to the house. After lashing out at the police for yielding no results, she had been sedated. As Gabby went to Gwen's room, she was stopped by Darrell. She wished Trina was around, as she was the only one who could put him in his place.

"Fiona means everything to your friend," Darrell said.

"Umm… yes." Gwen had softened because of the child she had initially planned to use as ammunition. Gabby feared the monster that would emerge if Fiona didn't return alive.

"Then why don't you help Gwen?" Darrell asked.

"What do you mean?" Gabby asked, confused.

"There's something you and your friends are hiding. I understand it's a secret, but this secret might help us find Fiona."

"I…." As much as she wanted to help Gwen, she couldn't tell him what had happened with Greg.

"Stop fishing for what's not there."

Gabby sighed in relief as Darrell frowned at Trina's arrival. She made a mental note never to be alone with Darrell ever again.

"You're hiding something, and you know what that means? Obstruction of justice! How can I find the child if you're not telling me the truth?" Darrell snapped.

"Stop creating stories in your head," Trina said sweetly.

"And stop interfering in my investigation! What were you doing at Solutions?"

"Go check on Gwen," Trina said to Gabby as she glared at Darrell.

Gabby was more than glad to leave them. She hurried to Gwen's room, where she found her friend getting out of bed and wearing a dazed look.

"It's you," Gwen said disappointedly.

"Yes. Do you know anything about Leah's past?" Gabby asked.

Gwen shook her head. "I know her marriage with Robert was on the brink of collapse. Robert's family tolerated her, but Blake disliked her a lot. He never told me why. He just spoke in parables."

"I've noticed the tension in the air whenever I've seen Blake and Leah together."

"Too bad he's not around. You and Trina might do better getting a straight answer from him than I did, but he's in Flint for some show." Gwen covered a yawn.

Gabby frowned. Flint? "Are you sure about that? Because I saw him a few days ago."

Gwen rolled her eyes. "He's been in Flint for almost a month. He left almost after Fiona's birth; he brought the huge pink teddy bear for her." Tears welled in her eyes, and Gabby hugged her comfortingly.

"Umm… so he never told you why he disliked Leah?" Gabby asked.

"No, and I don't care. All that matters now is finding Fiona."

Their conversation was cut short when the butler brought in a trolley filled with lunch, so Gabby went downstairs. She ran into Trina, who was flirting with one of the officers. Gabby pulled her aside.

"What is it?" Trina asked, seeing the worry on her face. "Remember Blake?"

"Who's that?"

"Gwen's nephew-in-law, the one who hates Leah's guts," Gabby said.

"Umm… yeah, what about him?"

"Gwen said he's in Flint, but I swear I saw him at the pharmacy a couple of days ago." Gabby had gone to pick up some vitamins and had seen him. He'd left so quickly that she hadn't had a chance to say hello.

"Why would he lie about not being in town? I don't think he's even dropped by since the kidnapping," Danielle said, joining them and catching the last bits of the conversation.

"And Gwen has no idea why this Blake dude hates Leah?" Trina asked.

"She doesn't know." Gabby shook her head. "Hmm…."

"What?" Gabby asked, seeing that spark of excitement in Trina's eyes.

"We're pretty sure Leah didn't act alone. She had an accomplice.

What if…?"

"No way! Blake?" Danielle shook her head.

Gabby gave her a long look. "You should know by now that anything is possible." After what they had gone through in the past, she wouldn't put it past him.

"Exactly! We need to find out if he is indeed in town. Danielle, can you get his home address?" Trina asked.

"Yeah, my cousin hangs around with him. I can also ask a few questions about Blake's dislike for Leah."

"He's watching us," Gabby said as they headed out. She groaned as Trina turned around and waved at Darrell.

Danielle's cousin, Mack, gave them Blake's address but told them Blake was in Flint. Last night, he uploaded a picture of himself at a bar with his friends.

"Do you know why he dislikes Leah?" Danielle asked.

Mack, who was on speakerphone, asked, "Who's Leah?"

"His uncle's ex-wife married Robert before Gwen," Danielle said. "Oh, that old broad. I don't know. I think they were kind of close when we were younger, but shit just happened, and he was pissed with her. I don't know what went down. I asked him a couple of times, but he didn't answer. Do you need anything else? 'Cause, this chick is with me, and she's ready for action."

"Thanks, Mack, and be safe. Remember to use a—"

The ladies laughed at the dial tone while Danielle rolled her eyes. "I was just being a caring aunt," Danielle mumbled.

"I'm sure he knows all the means of protection out there, Danielle. I'm curious about what caused the fallout between Leah and Blake," Gabby said.

"We'll find out," Trina said with determination.

Blake lived in a luxury high-rise building. An acquaintance of Danielle's stayed there, and they could gain entrance. However, they headed for the fifth floor and went to Blake's apartment.

There was no response after three knocks. Just as they were about to knock again, the neighbor next door, a skinny dude who reeked of cigarettes, walked out. He held on to a girl covered in tats.

"He ain't around. He went to Paris or some shit like that," the dude said.

"And he hasn't been around since?" Trina asked. "Naah," the dude drawled.

"I told you I heard someone in there two days ago," the girl said as they headed toward the elevator.

"You were high, babe," the guy replied.

"Well, no one seems to be home," Gabby said as Trina pulled a bobby pin out from under her wig and tried to pick the lock. In less than five minutes, Trina was able to unlatch the lock, and they were in.

Blake's apartment had a minimalist style, with black, white, and brown designs. Artwork lined the walls of the living room.

"Let's spread out and make this quick," Trina said, heading toward a corridor.

A few minutes later, they met in the living room. Trina shook her head. "The boy is damn neat. Everything is so organized. I couldn't find anything."

"I didn't find anything either," Gabby sighed.

"I don't know, but I found this in the trash." Danielle held a packet. Gabby frowned as she stared at it. It was for a spy cam. "It might not mean anything; he was probably spying on a girl or something."

"Oh my God!" Gabby went pale as an idea struck her. "What is it?" Trina asked.

"Before he left, Blake took a teddy bear to Gwen's place. You know, the big pink one?" The ladies nodded; they knew the one she was referring to. It was in Fiona's room. "I know it doesn't seem out of place, but what if there's a spy cam in the bear?"

"Fuck!" Trina grabbed the packet from Gabby. She pulled out her phone from her purse and googled the brand name. "Damn!" She shoved the phone into Gabby's face. The particular brand was used as a teddy cam.

"Wait! So does this mean Blake kidnapped Fiona? Why

would he even do such a thing?" Danielle cried.

"Because Leah made him do so. Whatever she has on him must be big," Trina said. "But the kid isn't home. There are no traces of any baby things here. He has to be elsewhere. Call Gwen and ask her if his parents are in town and if they have a home around here or something."

Gabby made the call. Gwen sounded disoriented. She didn't give her their theory because she knew how crazy Gwen would react.

After hanging up, she turned to the other ladies and relayed the information she had learned. "Blake's parents are in Portugal. They have a house a few minutes from here, near the pharmacy where I saw Blake."

"Then let's go!" Trina said, hurrying toward the door.

CHAPTER EIGHT

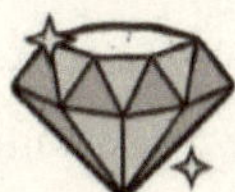

TRINA, DANIELLE, & GABBY

The ladies had been parked outside Blake's parent's house for over an hour. They had noticed no signs of life, and Trina felt it was too risky to search the property. It was large, and they could raise suspicion.

Danielle covered a yawn. She was tired of sitting in a cramped vehicle when she could be elsewhere—in the office, at home, or with Brad. Sitting here while night drew closer seemed a waste of time.

"Trina, how long are we—" She stopped as a man emerged from the house with a hood covering his head. He glanced left and right as if looking out for someone. A cab drew next to him, and he quickly got in.

"Well, I'll be damned," Gabby said.

"There's only one explanation for his erratic behavior," Trina said. "He's hiding something. But... but...." Danielle wasn't sure what else to say.

"I need to get into the house," Trina said, reaching for the door. "Hey!" Danielle pulled her back. "You can't just go in there. You don't know what you'll encounter!"

"So? We can sit out here doing nothing. Fiona could be in there." Trina opened her black bag. She handed some headphones to Danielle and Gabby before pulling out her gun.

Gabby's heart began to pound. As if having a premonition, she felt something terrible was about to happen.

"Trina, I think we should call the cops," Danielle suggested.

Trina gave her a haughty look. "We can't wait for the cops to get here. Besides, what would we tell them, huh? Look, stay out here, be on the lookout, and I'll go in there." She stepped out of the car.

"Be safe, Trina," Danielle cautioned; however, Trina was already jogging toward the house. Danielle turned to Gabby, who wore a worried look. "I have a bad feeling about this."

"Me too. I'm going to call Gwen. She needs to get up here," Gabby said, already dialing Gwen.

Danielle hoped it wasn't going to be too late. She plugged in the earphones and talked to Trina as Gabby spoke quietly to Gwen.

"Trina, where are you?" Danielle asked.

"Going around the back of the house. The front door is locked." "Be careful. There might be a security alarm," Danielle warned.

A big house like this had to have an alarm system. A few moments later, she heard Trina curse. "What is it?" Danielle asked.

"The back door is locked. I should pick the lock," Trina said. "No! I'm pretty sure there's an alarm system. You're going to notify someone," Danielle advised.

"Don't worry; I'm going to be careful."

She could hear Trina breathing softly as she worked on the lock. "They're headed here. I'll take a leak behind one of the trees,"

Gabby said as she stepped out of the car.

"I'm in!" Trina said as the door made a creaking sound. Danielle heard her shuffle around, then "Fuck!"

"What is it?" Danielle asked, perking up. "There's a gun pointed at me."

A shocking rap on the window had Danielle looking up. She gasped. Blake had a gun to Gabby's head. He gestured at Danielle to get out of the car.

"Blake… umm… what are you doing here?" Danielle said as she stepped out.

"You guys should never have come here. You fell right into the trap," Blake spat.

"Blake, please just let us go. Please," Gabby begged. Danielle gasped as the gun touched her head.

"You!" Blake barked, nodding at Danielle. "Move! Move toward the house!"

Danielle did as instructed. However, she was scared for her friend's life. She had lost communication with Trina when she told Danielle a gun was pointed at her. What had happened to her?

"Knock on the door twice," Blake said.

After the second knock, the door was flung open. Danielle

wasn't surprised to see Leah standing there. The bitch was behind all of this, of course!

"Well, well. If it isn't Gwen's loser friends. Welcome, welcome."

Danielle gasped as Leah grabbed her arm, pulling her into the house.

"You're hurting me!" Danielle cried as the woman's fingers dug deeper into her skin.

"Shut up!" Leah snapped.

They were pulled past the living room and into a bedroom, and Danielle sighed in relief when she saw Trina. She was alive! But she was tied to a chair. Trina flashed her a smile. Her eyes shifted and rested on a cot. Inside was a baby. It was Fiona!

"You took Fiona!" Danielle spat.

Leah laughed, sending chills down her spine. "Of course I did.

Well, technically, Blake did, but on my orders."

Leah tossed her on a chair, tying her up as Blake did the same to Gabby. Leah stepped back and gave a little clap.

"This is just so great! The only person missing is Gwen, and then the party will begin!" Leah smiled.

"You're crazy!" Gabby spat, then yelped as Leah struck her face. "I'm crazy? Why wouldn't I be crazy when my husband traded me for a freaking spoiled brat? He embarrassed me! Made a fool of me! Everyone laughed at me! He went for that brat. The fucking brat who treated me with disrespect," Leah yelled.

Indeed, Gwen had treated Leah with disrespect, but that

was just Gwen's character. And as much as that could be said to be a catalyst for Leah's behavior, it seemed Gwen had seen through Leah's facade from the beginning.

"Robert was my first love. We had been together since we were children! Children! And he traded me for her? He gave up our love and the promises he made, and you dare call me crazy?"

"Do you prefer a woman scorned?" Trina asked with a shrug. Leah flashed angry eyes at her. "Do you think this is funny?" "No, I don't. I think it's pathetic. Men leave the women they build empires with every day, but that doesn't mean you get to kidnap a child. Take your divorce package, get yourself a young man, and live a great life. But you chose to stay and get entangled in Robert and Gwen's lives. You had the choice to move on. This is on you. Don't blame anyone but yourself."

Leah moved closer to Trina, and Danielle's eyes widened in fear. The woman glared down at Trina. "Your friend ruined my marriage! She took away my happiness. And for that, I will take away *her* happiness." "You're only angry because she gave Robert a child, something you could never give."

The sadness quickly vanished, replaced by anger, as she struck Trina in the face. "Gwen deserves everything that is happening to her!" Leah spat.

"And Blake, how does he come into the equation?" Trina asked with a nod at the silent man in question.

Leah laughed. "I guess none of you saw it coming that Blake would be involved in this. He's the person least expected."

"I thought you hated her guts, Blake," Gabby said.

"Oh, he does." Leah smiled as Blake glared at her. "But you see, I have something against him. A long time ago, when Blake was seventeen, he got involved with a girl and her friend. There was alcohol and, of course, cocaine. And somehow, she overdosed. He called his aunt for help."

"I regret calling you." Blake shook his head.

"It's too late for regrets. You would still be behind bars now if I hadn't helped get rid of the bodies."

"Bodies?" Danielle squeaked.

Leah shrugged. "The other girl was too stoned to realize what was happening. And since then, he has been indebted to me."

"You have taken advantage of me all these years because of a mistake I made as a teenager!"

She silenced him by placing a finger over his lips.

Danielle felt like puking; she had a feeling one of the advantages involved sexual favors. This woman was vile! Gwen was right in treating her unfairly.

Leah laughed. "For so long, I have wanted to get rid of Gwen. Do you know how many times I have tried in the past several years, but she has escaped me? The car would refuse to start when she was meant to get involved in an accident. She wouldn't take the stairs when I loosened the boards. Nothing seemed to work. But I never gave up. And then she got pregnant. She would give Robert the only thing I couldn't," Leah said with a faraway look.

"And you decided not to hurt her until she gave birth to the child," Gabby said.

Leah nodded. "It was the perfect time to get rid of Gwen. She was so vulnerable when pregnant. But I wanted Robert and me to have a child. It didn't matter if it came from that brat, so my plan began to slow its pace."

"You decided to fake having cancer so you wouldn't be suspected when the kidnapping finally happened," Danielle said, putting things together.

Leah smiled her way, but only for a second. Then a scowl replaced it. "But Gwen had to ruin my plan. With your help, of course! But I never gave up; I stayed in the shadows, watching, preparing for my day of victory."

"So, what's the next plan? Do you think Robert will get back to you because you have his child?" Trina asked.

"The next plan is to get rid of Gwen for good, and then, while Robert mourns the death of that brat, I'll step in and be the mother to his child and the woman who has always loved him."

"And how are you going to kill Gwen? She's not stupid, you know," Danielle said.

"I admit, she isn't stupid, but she trusts the three of you, just as she trusted Blake, letting him into her home so he could spy on them, allowing us to strike at the perfect moment."

"So that's how you knew the routine, the spy cam," Danielle said. Leah's eyes flashed. "How did you figure that out? It doesn't even matter. I have always disliked the three of you. I will be getting rid of you all anyway. You thought you were smart, but we figured you would discover the truth and try to play heroes. You have no idea how delighted I was when I saw your car out there."

"Hey, what're you doing!" Gabby cried as Leah began to check her pockets. She pulled away with her cell phone.

"You're going to call Gwen and tell her to come here. Alone. You will tell her that you found Fiona and she must come here. Understand?"

"I'm not going to—Okay!" Gabby relented as Leah pointed a gun at her head.

"Umm… Leah?" Blake called. He was standing by the window. "What?" Leah snapped.

"You need to see this." Blake's voice was filled with fear.

Leah hurried over to the window. There was rage in her eyes when she turned to them. "How did the cops get here? Who told them?"

The captives remained quiet.

"I asked a question! Who told them we're here?" Leah snapped. They were still quiet.

"You want to do this the hard way?" Leah asked as she walked to the cot.

Danielle gasped as she pointed the gun at the child. "Leah, what are you doing?" Blake cried.

"I'm not going to go down without causing Gwen sorrow she can never recover from. If I have to kill the baby, I will!" Leah spat with fury.

"You said she wasn't going to get hurt. You promised, Leah.

Please, Leah, don't hurt the child!" Blake pleaded.

"He's right! The baby is innocent in all of this," Trina added.

Leah glared at Trina. "I don't care! I will not lose this fight.

Gwen must pay for her atrocities!"

"Drop the gun!" Blake said, pointing a gun at Leah.

Danielle gasped. If she survived this, she was going far away on vacation to a place free from guns and crazies.

"You're stupid, Blake! You're involved in this as well. We can't go down without a fight!"

"I can't let you hurt the baby. I can't. Drop the g—"

Danielle yelled as a gun went off, and Blake slumped to the ground.

"Oh my God!" Gabby cried before puking.

Leah smiled at them. "Nothing will stand in my way. Nothing! I don't care who I have to kill or destroy; Gwen must feel my pain."

Simultaneously, there was banging at the front and back doors. "Give it up now, Leah," Trina said in a stern voice. "The cops will be here in a few seconds."

"I will only give up when I'm dead." Leah aimed the gun at a now- stirring Fiona.

Gabby gasped as Trina flew out of her chair, tackling Leah to the ground. The gun slid from Leah's hold, close to Danielle's feet. Leah and Trina exchanged looks and dived for the gun, knocking Danielle and the chair to the ground. She gasped in pain as her head hit the floor.

"You fucking bitch!" Trina yelled as she struck Leah.

Danielle gasped as another gunshot went off. And then came a scream. She couldn't see anything in the position she was in.

The door burst open as armed cops rushed into the room. She heard a series of commands and a call for medical help.

Two officers helped Danielle up, and she was untied. She looked around and gasped. "Trina!"

Her friend lay in a pool of blood next to Leah, with a knife protruding from her stomach. Danielle ran to Trina but was held back by an officer as Trina received first aid. Tears rolled down her cheeks. For the first time in what seemed forever, she muttered a prayer on behalf of Trina.

CHAPTER NINE

TRINA & GWEN

Trina had a banging headache. It felt like some bastard had run her over! She turned to the other side but stopped as pain spread through her arm. What the hell! Then it all came flashing back to her. She tackled Leah to the ground and stabbed her with the knife she had pulled from her pocket to free herself from the ropes. The gun had gone off, and that fucking bitch had shot her!

A noise sounded, bringing her back to the present, and her eyes flew open. Her gaze immediately locked on to the most irritating, dark eyes.

"I told you not to interfere in my case," Darrell said with a scowl. "What the hell? Are you fucking nuts?" She struggled against the handcuff, securing her wrist to the side of the bed.

"Darrell, leave the woman alone!" Robert scolded as he walked in, followed by Gwen holding her baby.

"Fiona?"

"Yes. She's okay and alive because of you. No harm was

done to her." Gwen smiled with tears in her eyes.

Trina barely held in her tears as she stared at the sleeping beauty.

"Thank you, Trina. You risked your life for our daughter, and we are forever indebted to you," Robert said tenderly.

"Tell this idiot to get the cuffs off me!" Trina snapped. "Darrell." Robert gave the younger man a warning look.

The asshole took his time removing the cuffs, and she glared at him as she attempted to massage her wrist, which was difficult since her other arm was in a sling.

"It's not bad. More like a scratch, but you lost some blood," Gwen informed her. "You might be out of work for a month, though," she said with a shrug.

"Hey! A month!"

"That's what you get for trying to save your goddaughter." Gwen smiled.

Trina chuckled. So, she now had a goddaughter? She gladly accepted the position. Her humor suddenly slid away. "What about…?"

"She's dead," Gwen said distastefully. "She didn't make it to the hospital."

"She's lucky she's dead. Otherwise, I would have killed her myself," Robert grumbled.

Trina believed him. He might have cared for Leah, but she crossed the line with what she did to his family.

"And Blake?"

"He's dead too. However, he was able to give testimony before he died," Darrell informed her.

Damn! That must suck. "I'm sorry about him," she said to

the couple.

Robert shook his head. "I can't believe Leah had been taking advantage of him all these years. I was married to that woman for a long time, but she never hinted at how vile she was."

"She was crazy." Trina was glad the bitch was dead and Fiona was back with her parents.

"There are some questions I have to ask you," Darrell said.

Trina threw him a glare while Robert said, "Come on, Darrell, give the woman a break!"

"But—"

"Robert, why don't you two go for a stroll? Send Danielle and Gabby in," Gwen said while rocking Fiona.

Immediately the room cleared out, and Gwen hugged Trina. "I don't know what I would have done if I had lost her," Gwen said as a tear slid down her cheek.

"Gwen, you're crying. I need a camera for this," Trina teased. Gwen glared at her as she pulled away. "Thank you." She smiled.

Trina could feel the shift in their relationship. The women may annoy her and all that, but she cared for them more than any of her other friends. It was funny how all of this had started with an invite to a tea party, and now she was practically friends for life with them. Trina, Gwen, Danielle, and Gabby had gone through a lot in the past year, which only strengthened their bond. All the billionaires' women.

"Trina!" Gabby cried, running to her side, Danielle fast behind her.

"You scared us so much!" Danielle added.

"It'll take more than a bullet to stop me," Trina said, making everyone laugh.

"Whew! I'm so glad this is over. Remember the dream I told you guys about?" Gabby began.

Gwen rolled her eyes. "Your stupid dream started all of this. No more dreams, all right?"

"I didn't even ask; how did the cops know where we were?" Trina asked.

Gabby smiled sheepishly. "I called Gwen when you were getting into the house. Thank goodness you weren't your petty self, asking ridiculous questions," she directed at Gwen.

"At that moment, I could doubt anyone. I alerted Darrell, and the rest is history," Gwen said.

"At least he's good for something," Trina said. "I fear how things would have gone if Leah had gotten you to come over alone." Leah would not have hesitated in getting rid of them in her twisted plan to be with Robert and raise baby Fiona.

"If anything had happened to me, I swear I would have haunted her from my grave. I'm so glad this is over. I'm not letting my child out of my sight. Not even for a second!" Gwen said with firmness.

Gwen was going to be more protective, and it was well deserved.

She had gone through hell with her daughter's disappearance.

The ladies had to be chased out by the nurses before they would leave. They spent the hours up to that point talking about almost everything. There was calm among them, which Trina was grateful for. Their lives prior to her arrival had been going well, but eventually, they would have ended up frustrated. She had given them confidence and made them realize the power of being a woman.

Danielle was an active member of her company and was back with her husband. Whatever decision she made concerning her marriage was up to her, and Trina knew she would make the best one for herself now that she knew her worth.

Gwen was the mother to Trina's goddaughter and was married to a man who loved her. She was a spoiled brat but a darling who made a great friend.

Gabby would be a mother in a few months, her wish finally being fulfilled. She had a great support system in her husband, Dave. They all had a long way to go, but they had a great starting point.

As for Trina, her business was going well. As the hospital room's lights went off, she decided perhaps it was time for her to open her heart. She decided to call Detective Darrell.

ABOUT THE AUTHOR

Tina Luckett is from Van Buren Township, Michigan. She is a U.S. Army veteran with a heart of gold and a natural desire to experience life to its fullest. Tina earned her Master of Science degree in Administration - Leadership from Central Michigan University. With a career spanning decades, Tina has accumulated a lifetime of experiences allowing her to write her novels.

Tina is married to her best friend of over 33 years and has two adult daughters they raised with the same decency and thoughtfulness as they treat others.

Tina has been a lifelong writer. Her first book, The Suite Tea Society, The Boss Moves Series continues gaining popularity and, she hopes, brings readers the same levels of happiness as she feels today.

Follow Tina on Social Media:
Website: www.TinaLuckett.com
Email: TinaLuckett7@gmail.com
IG: @TinaLuckettBooks
FB: @Lucketteer